This book is a work o' imagination. All names, characters, events, places, products etc. have been used for this fictional purpose. If, by chance, they or it resembles someone or something; living or dead, it is by coincidence. All scriptures are taken from the Bible and is not the work of the author.

*** Although this is Christian Fiction, there is some mentions of foul language. ***

Published by: Twins Write 2 Publishing

© 2022 by Lakisha Johnson

All rights reserved

Almost Destroyed

When she's had enough

dedication

This book is dedicated to the woman or man whose been almost destroyed by the strains and struggle of life. To you who's had to fight every freaking day to survive, this book is for you. While this may be fiction, I pray something written on these pages will give you strength to press through and hope again.

gratitude

I'll always begin by thanking God. It's Him who believes enough in who He created to trust me with this gift. This is why, even when its hard and doesn't pay off like I expect, I'll never give up. Each day, I accept this gift, proudly and unapologetically serving God through the pages of a fiction book.

To my entire family, know I love each of you for supporting me, release after release.

To my sister Laquisha and my girl, Shakendria ... thank you for always being willing to help me on this tedious journey.

To each of you who support Lakisha, the PreacHER, Author and Blogger ... THANK YOU! I wouldn't be who I am without you who purchase, download, recommend and review my books. Please, don't stop believing in me. We're connected now and that makes us family.

disclaimer

Trigger Warning: Ava's story is one of abuse, anger, and pain as she takes this journey of healing. Reading her story may trigger unresolved emotions and pain for you. Guard yourself and your heart. If this means you are unable to read this, I understand and pray one of my other books will be a better fit.

Here's the link to my website.

www.authorlakishajohnson.com

Also, this is a work of Christian Fiction and within this book is prayers, scriptures, sermons, and a whole lot of God. There's also cursing because we're dealing with imperfect people and the raw emotions of anger. If these are the kinds of things you don't like to read and will cause you to leave a low review, I implore you to return this book.

For me, this isn't simply writing, it's ministry and sometimes ministry isn't confined to tradition. Yes, I get its Christian Fiction and most desire it to be "clean," but sometimes, we have to meet people where they are and unfortunately, it may be a place of darkness and pain.

Nonetheless, if you're deciding to read on, HAPPY READING and I hope you enjoy it. – Lakisha

Almost Destroyed

When she's had enough

chapter one

"Dang girl, I see you." I say smiling to myself while turning in the mirror.

"You still fat." Andre laughs out loud while walking by.

"It's you're dummy." I yell before continuing to admire the 50 pounds and three dress sizes I've lost over the last year. I finish getting dressed as my phone vibrates with a message from June, my boss's admin, and friend.

June Coleman: There's a staff meeting at 9 AM sharp. Do not be late!

I lock the phone and start to grab my things.

"I need fifty dollars." Andre stops me in the hallway.

"What does that have to do with me?"

"Ava, please don't get cussed out this morning."

"Andre, please don't get punched this morning. Now, move. I have a meeting."

"Not looking like that. No wonder them folk won't promote you. Whales should not be dressing in multiple colors and heels, come on sis, really?" he circles me. "Girl, they're screaming to be set free. And red lipstick. No honey." He laughs.

"Oh, I guess you're the new queen of fashion?"

"I got your queen."

"Just so you know. I was promoted a year ago with a huge raise and the only one complaining about how I look is you. Besides, you seem to like whale meat seeing you're still placing your head between my thick thighs every chance I allow your bob the builder, square back, hoof foot having ass. While you're worried about my promotion, focus on moving up the rank, Mr. fifteen year, beat cop."

His hands ball into fist.

"Oh, you're mad?" I laugh. "Then stop dishing out what you can't take. You're always degrading and talking about me like I don't have feelings. Negro, you aren't a prize either. We both know the only reason you haven't left is because nobody will take care of your trifling ass. I've been the only fool to stay."

"Then I guess we're both losers."

"Not for long." I look at my watch and see it's 8:30. "Crap. Move, before I'm late."

I grab my bag and rush out the door. Twenty-seven minutes later, I walk into the office to June grabbing my bags and pushing me into the meeting.

"Good morning," my boss Winston Paxton Sr. says from the front of the room giving everyone a moment to settle down. "I know this meeting was last minute, but something has come up we couldn't put off any longer."

He pauses looking over at his son who has a smirk on his face. "Over the last six months, there have been major changes happening behind the scenes. I thought I could prevent them from affecting all of you, at least until the end of the year but—" he chokes up.

"Don't worry Pops, I got this." Winston Jr., states touching his arm. "What my father is trying to say is, he's retiring and there will be changes in personnel starting today. In other words, most of you will not be employees after this."

Everyone begins to shift in their chairs. Winston Jr. has been waiting to get his hands on this company since he turned eighteen, three years ago. He nods to June, and she begins handing out envelopes. When she stops in front of me, I see tears sliding down her face. Grabbing it, I can no longer hear what Winston Jr. is saying as I tear it open to find separation papers and a severance packet. I don't wait for him to finish. I get up from my chair and it rolls back into the wall causing everybody to look at me as I storm out the conference room.

"Ava, wait." Winston Sr. calls out.

I stop and he comes around to face me.

"I'm so sorry about this. I did everything possible to keep you on, but Junior wants an entirely different leadership staff."

"I understand." I lie.

"You've been one of my best employees and if there's anything I can do to assist you in finding another career, please don't hesitate to call. You have my personal cell number." He kisses me on the cheek before whispering in my ear. "I did give you the biggest severance I could."

"Mr. Paxton, I really appreciate all you have done for me these past thirteen years. You gave me a chance when no one else would and I'll never forget it. I hope you'll enjoy retirement and whatever else the future holds for you." I hug him. "As for Winston Jr., he can kick rocks."

He laughs and I hurriedly walk away before the tears start. Standing at the door of my office, I see everything is already packed. I glance around, remembering how I began at the bottom of this company, literally. It didn't matter I had a bachelor's degree. I was a black girl from Alabama, straight out of college with no corporate work experience and no one was willing to give me a chance. I needed a job and the only position I could get was working in housekeeping, cleaning up after hours.

From there it was the mail room, filing clerk and administrative assistant until I found out they offered tuition assistance. I took advantage of it. One night, I ran into Mr. Paxton when he was leaving and asked why it was so hard for women to move up in this company. He didn't have an answer. Finding out I was back in school to get my master's degree, he promised me a job as an Associate when I graduated. He kept it. Over the years, I worked my way up to senior level. Although I knew the day would come for his son to take over, I wasn't expecting it to be today.

I grab the box with my personal items, stop by June's desk to get my purse and leave the company's computer. Hitting the button for the elevator, I turn to give the office one last glance. Making it to my truck, I thank God, I paid it off when I did because when all else fails, I have her. I get in but before pulling out, I open the severance packet.

It's a check for $16,427.01 after taxes, a recommendation letter, and six months of insurance benefits.

"Thank you, Jesus." I exclaim

chapter two

I stop by the credit union and open a new account to deposit the check. One Andre won't know about. Years ago, I made the mistake of adding him to my checking account and since I can't close the old one, without him, a new one it is. After transferring most of the money from the old to the new, I remove my name from that account.

Afterwards, I get a large cookie crumble frappe from Starbucks to toast the end of what was and the beginning of what is. Forget the calories. Taking the scenic route home, I turn into this new subdivision I've been watching the last year. The condos are outside of my price range, but it doesn't keep me from dreaming with my eyes open.

I drive by the first one built.

"Any day Lord." I whisper.

Continuing to drive the neighborhood, I park and walk into the model home.

"Good morning, welcome to Roundtree Estates. Is there anything I can help you with?" the agent asks standing from the desk.

"Good morning and no ma'am, I'm only looking."

"Well, if you'd like I can give you the tour. My name is Katrina Gaskins."

"Ava Gentry." I reply, noting she's new and doesn't know I've toured this house seven times. Smiling, I allow her to excitedly show it to me again.

"As you can see, the amenities of the condos are amazing. The builder is pulling out all the stops to ensure even the smallest of details are met without breaking your pocket. Anyway, these are French style condominiums that comes standard with granite countertops and stainless-steel appliances, color customized to your liking. The great room has wood flooring, stacked stone fireplace and custom built-ins."

I follow her to the master bedroom admiring the walk-in closets and walk-through shower in the bathroom.

"This space can be used for an office, shoe closet or—

"Prayer room." I cut in referring to the extra room.

She smiles. "Yep, that too. Would you like to go upstairs?" she asks after we'd gone through the laundry room, screened in porch and back yard.

"No thanks. I've seen enough to already be in love."

"Are you looking to purchase soon?"

"Oh no. Just dreaming, but when I am, I hope to build just like this. The design is everything."

"Well, if you think this is something, you should see the home we're about to list. It's 2,846 square feet, four bedrooms, three-and one-half baths with an outdoor living space and an upstairs balcony overlooking downtown Memphis."

"The one at 4926 Whisper Hollow Cove?" I ask.

"Yeah, you've seen it?" she looks at me confused.

"I have." I admit. "Well, not the inside because I didn't think it was available and it's way out of my price range." I chuckle.

She smiles, grabbing her keys and cell phone from the desk. "Come on. There's nothing wrong with looking."

I follow her out the back door to a golf cart. She drives to the next street over.

"Wow, this is amazing. Do they all come with this amount of detail?" I ask walking through the front door.

"Not standard, but it's available for a little extra. However, and you didn't hear this from me. This one was designed by our builder for his fiancé, but she nixed it the moment she saw it."

"Really, why?"

"Let's just say, she was looking for something grander."

"Baby, I couldn't imagine not falling in love with this. This kitchen. Oh my God. A butler's pantry, pot filler and this stove."

I turn to see her looking with a huge smile.

"I love to cook, if it isn't evident by my size."

"Oh no ma'am. We're not doing that. You're beautiful and exactly how God created. Don't ever doubt the perfection you are, no matter your shape or size. Baby, haven't you heard, the greatest gifts are those in big packages. Well, I made that up, but hope it inspires you." She smiles.

I wipe across my eyes.

"I didn't mean to make you cry." She says coming over.

"It's been a rough morning."

"Can I pray for you?"

My eyes widen.

"I apologize if it isn't something you don't believe in."

"No, you can. It's just been a while since I've prayed or even talked to God." I admit.

"Then there's no time like the present to begin again."

She grabs my hands. "God, of Heaven and Earth, I come before your throne for my sister Ava. God, she's had a rough day and in need of you. It matters not the reason she turned away or time she's been gone, will you come and see about your child. God, when you show up grant her the forgiveness she desperately needs, give her new eyes to see the glory of you in her life and lead her back to the path and plans you have for her life. Father, I don't know why she's had to cry or what she stands in need of, but you do. This is why I'll ask you to break every stronghold, destroy every curse, remove her heart of stone, wipe away self-doubt and replace it with hope, close every door not meant and open what is. God, whatever darkness she's faced this morning, let her see it's not the end. In your name, we pray. Amen."

"Amen. Wow. I don't know whether to thank you or give an offering." I smile through tears.

"Ava, I don't know what you're blaming God for or the reasons you've turned away from Him, but He's still here. Try Him again." She pulls me into a hug. "Now, let's finish admiring this home."

She walks away like she didn't just wreck my spirit. I look up at the ceiling.

"Okay, God."

I take my time looking through every room. Walking into the master bedroom, I'm blown away. The colors are the exact ones I would choose.

"What do you think?"

"This feels like home."

"Ava, I know you said the condos are out of your price range, but have you started the process of being approved by a mortgage company?"

"Not yet and seeing I was laid off today, I'd have to wait a while to be approved."

"Delay is not denial. Do you mind if I ask you a personal question?"

"The way you just prayed for me. Girl, ask away."

"You said it's been a while since you've prayed. Does that mean you don't have a church home?"

"I don't."

"Our church, Repairers of the Breach Ministries, is having a three-night revival this week and I'd love if you'd come. You don't have to do all three nights, but I think you'll enjoy it."

"Sure. I'd love too."

"You would? Wow, that was easier than I expected."

"With the way my life is going, I need God."

"Take my number and text me. Afterwards, I'll send you the flier."

After exchanging numbers, I wave goodbye to Katrina, passing by the house again and slowing down. "One day Lord. One day."

chapter three

"Dear God, I know it's been a while since I've talked to you. Shoot, it's been a long time since I've done anything concerning you and I'm sorry. I allowed distractions to derail me from your plans for my life. Please forgive me." I exhale.

"I shouldn't even be asking anything of you, but if you find it in your heart, will you please take over my life. I'm tired of being like this. Whatever you have for me, show me. And God, before I go into another dark place, accept another position that may hurt me or wind up wasting more years in sin, shut my mouth. Before I make another bad decision by flesh, sit me down. I need you God and if you'll have me, I'm ready. Amen."

With time before church, I'm sitting at the kitchen counter with my laptop when Andre comes in.

"What did you cook?"

"Hey Ava, how was your day? Oh, it was kind of crappy. Aw, I'm sorry to hear that. What can I do to make it better? A hug will help." I sarcastically say as he removes and replaces the pot tops on the stove.

"Ava, I'm not in the mood to pacify your fat ass feelings. I've had a long day."

"So have I, but I'm not taking it out on you and the least you can do is not take your frustrations out on me."

"Did you have to search for a missing two-month-old baby whose father confessed to killing her and throwing her in a river?"

I gasp.

"I didn't think so. Not everything is about you." He screams slamming the door of the refrigerator and opening a beer.

"I never said it was and I'm sorry about the baby. Nonetheless, you aren't the only one whose day was crappy. I lost my job."

"Fan-fucking-tastic. Well, I hope you'll have your half of the bills come the end of the month. I'd hate for you to be unemployed and homeless. Ain't too many places someone your size can go."

"Wow."

I close the computer and grab my purse to head out.

"Where are you going?" he asks with his face scrunched up.

"Church."

He laughs sending beer flying across the kitchen from his mouth.

"You're kidding. You haven't been to church in years."

"I know, hence my obvious circumstance."

"What's that?" he questions.

"This."

"Sis, nobody is making you stay here. You do because nobody else wants you. The best thing to ever happen to your life, is me. You were living in a rooming house on Madison Avenue taking the bus to an hourly job cleaning up after people when I saved you."

"And here I thought you loved me." I shake my head. "However, allow me to correct you. You don't have the power nor power to save me. You may have taken me from a rooming house, but everything else, you will not get credit for. I worked my ass off to get where I am. My only mistake, staying where I'm not wanted or appreciated."

He laughs. "Oh, I appreciate the bills you pay, the food you buy and cook and the way you keep a house. As for love, you don't even love yourself. How can you expect someone else too?"

My eyes widen.

"Don't look shocked. It is what it is. Have a great time at church and tell Jesus I said what's up."

In the truck, a little way down the street, I pull over.

You don't even love yourself. How can you expect someone else too?

He was right. Somewhere along the way, I stopped loving myself. Maybe it was after learning my birth mother loved crack more than me. Maybe it was the physical abuse by my grandfather until I was eight. Maybe it was after the many foster homes that left me more abused and broken. Maybe it was after the second failed suicide attempt, waking up in another mental hospital, drugged up but never helped. Maybe it was after being raped by the social worker who was supposed to protect me or almost killed by a renter at the rooming house.

"Why am I bothering with church? God doesn't love me." I cry. "He can't love me. Nobody does. I don't even love me. Ugh." I hit the steering wheel.

A few seconds later my phone vibrates. Popping up on the truck's screen, I see the text from Katrina. Trying to press ignore, I hit read instead.

"Hey, I'll wait for you by the front entrance. Text me when you're walking in."

I sit for a few more minutes then put the truck in drive and follow the directions to the church. Before getting out, I look in the mirror to fix my face before texting Katrina. Stopping at the door of the church, I take a deep breath to calm the rapid beating of my heart.

"Ava, I'm so glad you came." She pulls me into a hug.

"I almost didn't." I truthfully tell her. "It seems like everything is against me."

"Child, that's the enemy trying to stop you from moving towards God. Don't fall for the schemes because you're stronger and wiser than you think you are. Otherwise, you wouldn't have made it tonight. Yet, you pushed past the hold of flesh. Hallelujah."

Taking my hand, she leads me into the sanctuary. The seat she chose is near the front and nervous is an understatement because it feels like everyone's eyes is on me.

Katrina touches my leg and smiles. "No one is looking at you. You're safe here."

I smirk, nod and slink into the seat.

"Good evening mighty people of God." The guest speaker says from the pulpit. "Anybody else glad to be in the house of the Lord on a Wednesday night? I don't know about you, but I've lived long enough to know tomorrow isn't promised. So, if I can give God praise on a Wednesday for all He's done, I will. See, a few years ago, you couldn't pour church on me. I was a wretch undone, not fitting to live and too afraid to die. I was caught up in the enemy's trap and it was bad y'all.

He was my dealer, and I was eager to get to him, but how many of you know, drugs weren't my vice, neither was alcohol. What the enemy had me strung out on was sin and I wasn't even good at it. I'd come down off my high and be laying in the middle of my bathroom floor, naked and crying out to God like it was His fault. I'd be sobbing so hard, words barely audible, making no sense and blaming God when truth is, it wasn't God. It was my silly self.

I was the one who kept playing patty cake with the enemy, pacifying my pain with temporary pleasure that could satisfy my flesh. Every chance I got, I laid in beds of sin getting pleasured physically while dying spiritually and still blaming God. In debt and the reason the sheriff's deputy would knock on the door with an eviction notice, yet I'd blame God.

Oh, I know I'm not the only one. You can sit there and act like you've always been highly favored, but baby I've been messed up, tore up, raggedy, filthy, and downright disgusting. I wasn't worthy of God's restoration, yet when I repented, He kept His promise. All I had to do was own up to the fact, it wasn't God, it was me. And I came tonight with God's word of hope for those of you who've been in my shoes. You know, blaming God for being in the mess you're in when it isn't Him, it's you. Go with me to Isaiah, the fifty-ninth chapter and verses one through fifteen."

"Wow." I say to Katrina as we're walking out of the church.

"I know. That message was heavy, but right on time. Girl, how many times do we blame God for the stuff we get ourselves into when the whole time it's not God, it's us." She says referring to the Pastor's message title.

"Too many to count or admit." I reply making it to my truck.

"Ava, I'm glad you came tonight."

"I am too because I needed that kick in the butt." I laugh. "The day I met you, I'd just lost my job. Not to mention, I've been in a dead-end relationship far too long and I have no joy, nothing to smile about, my hope has dwindled, and self-esteem is shot. I was blaming God when it's been me this entire time. Man, I've made a mess of my life."

She lifts my head. "Now that you've taken responsibility, give God the shame of everything you're carrying around. Ava, God hasn't forgotten you. No matter what we go through, the multiple times we shut Him out and turn our backs, He's still there. It's like putting a call on hold. If you were to click back over, you'd realize God never hung up. Corny, I know."

"No, it makes perfect sense. Thank you, Katrina. I'll see you tomorrow night."

chapter four

The following week, I feel refreshed. After the three-night revival with Katrina, I've made up my mind to make major changes in my life. Starting with clicking back over to get God off hold. Second thing, ending this relationship with Andre.

Coming out of the guestroom where I moved after our last argument, He's standing there with a huge grin on his face.

"What's wrong with you?"

"Can't a man be happy to see his girlfriend?"

"Now, I'm girlfriend instead of whale." I chuckle proceeding into the kitchen. "Okay Andre. Besides, that smile looks like you have gas not happiness."

"You know—" he stops and takes a deep breath. "Ava, because I forgot Valentine's Day, I cooked dinner to make up for it. I know you like to eat."

"No thank you."

I see him twist the towel in his hands.

"Will you please sit down?"

"Andre, I don't have time for your games and whatever you're about to ask me for the answer is no."

"You haven't even had the honey-garlic salmon. Baby, this is me extending an olive branch."

"Oh, an olive branch instead of an apology. No, thanks."

"Please give me a chance." He smirks walking up to me. "Babe, I know things have been rough with us for a while, but I want things to change." He kisses my neck. "I really like having you here."

I push him away. "You like having me here. Dude, bye and stop calling me babe. We've been in this um, I don't even know what to call it, but it's been long enough to be pass liking."

"What more do you want from me?" he yells throwing the towel.

"Absolutely nothing."

"Then why are you mad?"

"I'm mad because of what I've allowed you to do to me. But this," I point between me and him, "it's over. I've accepted the disrespect, belittling, name calling and cheating. You only do things like this when you want something from me, not because you have genuine feelings towards me. Why was I never enough or worthy of you loving me?"

"Here we go." He scoffs. "It must be that time of the month. Forget about this and I'll ask you again in five days."

"No, it's not that time of the month, you asshole. I'm tired of being treated like trash. You give everybody else respect, except me. But who has been here with you through everything? When you were shot, who nursed you back to health? When you almost lost your job because of your drinking, I was here. Yet, you've never been here for me. I lost our baby, and you didn't even bother to leave work."

"What was I supposed to do?"

"Show up." I scream. "All I've ever wanted you to do was show up. Andre, I can't even count on you when I have a flat tire."

"You want to know why I do the things I do? It's because, never mind. I don't think you're ready to hear the real. So, go on to your room and pull your bag of snacks from under the bed and eat yourself into a diabetic coma. I'll see you in two days when you decide to come out."

"No, be a man and tell me."

"Ava, it's best you leave this alone before you get your feelings hurt."

"You don't care about my feelings, and this isn't the first time you've hurt them."

"Fine." He yells. "I do what I do because it's all you've ever required."

"What is that supposed to mean?" I question.

"When we met, you were unhealthy, unkept, and uncertain of your future. You were broken mentally, physically, and financially. You didn't have a pot to pee in or a window to throw it out off. You were shaken up from what happened at that rooming house and looking for the first thing to hitch your big ass too. You didn't require me to love you, nor treat you like you deserve, so I didn't. You didn't require love. You needed a safe place to stay, I gave you that. As for support, you didn't demand it either so why should I press the issue. You got exactly what you wanted which was a safe place to stay and a man. You can't cry foul on the play when you were the one who created the rules. Sweetie, you didn't start losing when you got with me, you've been lost all along."

I feel tears hitting the shirt.

"Man." He sighs. "I thought things were working fine between us and now you want to switch up. I'm sorry, but I can't offer you anything else. Look Ava, you're pretty for a big chick, you're smart and will work your ass off. One day you'll make a man, who chooses to love you, very happy. I'm not him. However, until you find somewhere else to stay, the guestroom is yours as long as your share of the bills are covered. Oh, I'll be okay with a little friend with benefit action too." He winks. "Whatever you decide, I'm cool with it, but I do need you to cosign for my new motorcycle. I left the application under your plate along with the job section from Sunday's paper. Good luck."

When he leaves, I feel myself getting sick. I race for the hall bathroom, barely making it to the toilet. Afterwards, I rinse my mouth and wash my hands. Staring at my reflection, I can't help but be angry with me because Andre is right. I allowed all of this. Sulking back to the bedroom, I lay across the bed.

"You've been losing all along. I do what I do because it's all you've ever required." I repeat Andre's words.

Angry, I go over to the closet and pull out my stash of calories. They are my go-to when I'm feeling down or depressed. Removing the top, I search through the powdered donuts, Lays and Barbeque potato chips, Oreos, Chips Ahoy, Cool Ranch Doritos, Ding Dongs, Almond Joys, Snickers and Air Heads.

Sitting inside the closet, I unwrap a snack cake and press it to my mouth before throwing it back inside and screaming.

"Forget this." I get up and begin pushing through the clothes. Settling on a black dress, I take it into the bathroom. A little while later, I walk inside Lottie's, a nightclub in North Memphis I overheard some old coworkers talking about.

"Dang, big momma, you wearing that dress. Let me buy you a couple of drinks to get you out of it later on." A random guy says causing the others around him to laugh.

I stop and look him up and down.

"Dude, you don't even have a print in the front of your pants, so I'm willing to bet whatever you got couldn't fit what I have under this dress anyway. Find somebody else to play with."

"I would say let's go out to my car to see, but you wouldn't fit into the backseat."

"Oh, you must be the one driving your grandmother's 2-door Pontiac I saw outside. Then you're right."

"Oooh." Some folks standing around laugh, making him mad.

"Somebody needs to teach you to stay in your place." He seethes.

"When you find somebody, I'll be at the bar."

"Fat bit—

"Is there a problem?" a guy interrupts standing next to me.

I look at him.

"No, lil dude was offering to get me drunk so he could remove my dress without consent before teaching me to stay in my place."

"Ray, you know we don't tolerate disrespect in this establishment. It's time you roll."

"Man, I was only playing with her insensitive ass. If you can't take jokes, stay at home."

"And if you don't know how to speak to women, stick talking to the guys."

"Let's go fellows."

"I apologize for that. My name is Chuck Laskey, the owner of Lottie's."

"Chuck, thanks for coming to my rescue, but I wasn't in danger, and I can fight my own battles. My name is Ava, by the way."

He holds his hands up smiling. "My bad. May I buy you a drink?"

"You sure can."

chapter five

Two hours later, I'm on the stage singing along with Tennessee Whiskey by Keke Wyatt.

"I've looked for love in all the same old places, found the bottom of a bottle is always dry. But when you poured out your heart, I didn't waste it, 'cause there's nothing like your love to get me high. You're as smooth as Tennessee whiskey, you're as sweet as strawberry wine. You're as warm as a glass of Brandy and honey, I stay stoned on your love all the time."

The few people left cheers as drunken tears stream down my face.

"You're as smooth as Tennessee whiskey. Tennessee whiskey. Tennessee whiskey." I take a bow and rush from the stage almost falling.

"Whoa." Chuck grabs me. "That was great. Hey, are you okay? Ava, talk to me."

I burst into uncontrollable sobbing.

"Come with me."

He leads me to a break room, handing me a bottle of water and sitting next to me. "You want to talk about it?"

"Have you ever felt so broken it made you feel like you were beyond repair? I have and it's at this very moment."

"Ava, the only person who can't be restored is a dead one." He grabs my arm, pressing two of his fingers on my wrist. "Yep, you're very much alive."

I look at him while the tears continue. "My life is a mess and here is it, 2 AM and I'm drunkenly sobbing in the presence of a stranger. Thank you for the drinks. I'm going to go."

I stand and quickly get dizzy falling into his lap. Without thinking, I kiss him.

"Ava, stop." He gently pushes me off.

"I get it. I'm not your type."

"No, you're not." He replies.

I shake my head. "Then why pump me full of drinks and wings if you didn't plan to take advantage of me?"

"I was being nice to a beautiful woman I felt needed a night out."

"Right." I drag out, chuckling. "You were being nice to a woman you've never met before. Yeah okay. Men are never just nice. There's always an ulterior motive. So, what is it? You want some head because you've heard big girls can do it good? No, it's money. You want money because I must be a miserable gullible fool, out on a

Tuesday night getting wasted? What do you want from me?" I yell.

"Ava, I don't know who hurt you, but it wasn't me and I will not apologize for the mistake of every man who has disappointed you. You are a beautiful woman, however you're not my type because I'm married and she's the only type I have. Also, if I wasn't married, I wouldn't take advantage of a woman who's clearly hurting. Here. Drink this water and let me get someone to take you home."

"I don't need your therapy, Dr. McStuffin or your pity. I got myself here, I can get home." I turn back to find my purse. "Where is my purse?"

The door closes.

"Where is my freaking purse and jacket?"

A few minutes later the door opens, and he comes in with a woman who's carrying my purse.

"Ava, this is my wife, Marcia." He kisses her on the cheek and closes the door.

"Here's your purse." She says extending her hand. "You left it at the bar."

I look up noticing she's the bartender. I take it, laying it in my lap.

"I'm sorry. I've made a fool of myself. Please forgive me."

She sits beside me. "Ava, we've all done some foolish things in our lifetime, yet it doesn't have to define who you are going forward. We all have a story, but you have to decide what you allow people to see and read."

"That's easier said than done when all you've ever had is bad. I mean look at me. It's a Tuesday night and I'm a mess, sitting in the back of a bar pouring my soul out to people I've never met before. I kissed your husband for God's sake then accused him of trying to take advantage of me. Why should I think he'd want somebody like me anyway?"

"Girl, life isn't your problem." She tells me.

"Then what is?"

"You are."

"Me?"

"Yes, you. Sure, you're in a bar on a Tuesday, but why couldn't you be here to enjoy the karaoke and margaritas, like everybody else instead of flashing this badge of shame and self-doubt."

"That's not what I'm doing."

"Of course it is. Ava, nobody is going to stop feeling sorry for you until you stop feeling sorry for yourself. How can you expect people to want more for you than you want for you? Okay, life has dealt you some bad hands, what else has life done because judging by the fact you're alive, healthy and in your right mind, it hasn't been all bad."

"How do you know?" I say with a little force. "You don't know me and what I've gone through?"

"Maybe not, but I know women like you. Those who've had to drag herself through life just to survive yet never feeling as though you are. A woman who no one has ever said was beautiful without a but afterwards. A woman who's had to prove herself over and over because of the color of her skin. A woman who was probably abused by a man, early in life and it set you up to distrust all men. A woman who can't even love her own body because nobody ever taught you too."

"Let me guess, you've been in my shoes?" I ask standing.

"No baby. I love me, always have and will. I don't have the testimony of having to find my voice, it was instilled in me from the time I could recognize my reflection in a mirror. I come from a long line of beautiful, black, big-boned women and it's been implanted in me to love every curve, stretch mark, dimple, pound, and ounce of me. I allow others to compliment me, but they surely don't validate me."

"Yeah, but you had somebody to do that for you, I didn't. While you were being taught to love you, my granddaddy was beating the crap out of me. He was mad for having to care for the child of his only daughter who was a crackhead. Listen, I thank you and your husband for the hospitality, but y'all don't know me and I definitely don't need the pity."

She chuckles. "Not everybody who offers help does it out of pity. There are still good people in the world Ava."

"Excuse me if I've never experienced them. Again, thanks."

"Will you at least let me take you home?" she asks.

"I'm good."

I walk out and realize the bar is empty besides the employees. Chuck is behind the bar and when he sees me, he stops. I get to the door and fumble trying to get it open.

"Please let me out of here."

"Hold on, ma'am." A gentleman says coming over.

Pushing the door open, he follows me out.

"What are you doing?" I abruptly turn to him.

"Walking you to your car. It's late." He replies looking confused. "Are you okay?"

"Peachy."

I hit the button to unlock my truck and get inside.

"You be safe getting home." He waves, backing away to watch me until I pull off.

chapter six

Hours later, I roll over cringing from the light and feeling for my phone on the nightstand. Instead my hand lands on something plastic. Opening my eyes, I see an iced honey bun, pineapple Fanta and note.

Ava,
I'm sorry for the things I said. I want you here and I love
you.
Andre.

I throw the paper down and sit up eyeing the honey bun and soda. Reaching for it, I quickly snatch my hand back.

"Life isn't my problem, I am."

I sit up, grabbing my head from the pounding happening inside. Dragging myself to the bathroom, I handle my hygiene, shower, and get dressed. Going into the kitchen, I swallow two extra-strength Tylenols with orange juice before heading back to the guestroom. Pushing through the headache, I pull out the tote of snacks from inside the closet dropping the honey bun and drink into it. Sliding my feet into Ugg boots, I carry it outside placing it on the curb in front of the house.

Making it back inside, I get my laptop and begin to search for apartments. An hour later, I've mapped out a plan for the day and decide to apply for some jobs. Logging into LinkedIn, I search for positions within my field of project management.

A listing pops up.

Senior Executive with Ruthie and Associates.

Curious, I click on the ad. "Must have senior experience in analytical work. I got that. A Master's Degree. I got that. Willing to travel. Hell yes." I excitedly read through the rest of the requirements. "Can't hurt to apply."

Two days later, I have my music on full blast while running on the treadmill. It stops when a call comes through from a number I don't recognize. I pause the treadmill and answer.

"This is Ava Gentry."

"Ms. Gentry, my name is Sharon Croswell and I'm calling about a position you applied for and after carefully reviewing your application, we'd like to move you to the next step in the hiring process. A face-to-face interview."

"Sharon, my apologies but I've applied for a few positions within the last couple of days. Can you tell me which one you're calling about?"

"No, I apologize for not stating it upfront. You applied for the position of Senior Executive with Ruthie and Associates. Are you interested, or shall I move on?"

"I am."

"Great. I will email you all of the details and please be on time."

She hangs up before I can reply but that doesn't stop me from doing a small happy dance before resuming my run. Getting home, the first thing I do is check my email, clicking the one from Sharon Croswell and reading it out loud.

"Ms. Gentry, thank you for your interest in the position of Senior Executive. Your official interview, which will include a drug test and thorough background check will be conducted Monday, February 22, 2021, at 8 AM. The address and parking details are listed below. The position pays an annual salary of $77,000 per year with bonus possibility. If you're no longer interested, please reply to this email, otherwise I look forward to seeing you. And I look forward to seeing you too sis." I squeal.

The day of the interview, I'm up before 6:30 AM. Coming out of the guestroom, Andre's door opens, and an unknown lady walks out buck naked.

"Oh, hey. My bad. Did we wake you?" she smiles looking back at Andre who's sprawled, on his back across the bed also naked.

"Tan, baby, go on and get me something to drink." He tells her. "Make sue you use plenty of ice."

"Sure thing love."

"Really Andre. What happened to, baby I want you here and I love you?" I mock.

"I do and I do, but a man has to eat, and you aren't putting out."

"And you wonder why. You bald face raccoon looking mother—you know what, you aren't even worth it." I walk off then double back. "I hope you catch herpes."

I go back into the room, slamming the door.

"Ugh." I angrily swipe the tears. "Why am I even crying over somebody who clearly doesn't respect me? It's obvious he never loved me. Who am I kidding? I've never truly loved me. A person who loves self doesn't keep subjecting themselves to this kind of pain. Lord." I pace around the room for a few minutes before deciding to pray. Kneeling beside the bed, I close my eyes.

"God, forgive me. I've messed up a lot in my life and here is another great example. I've failed you and me." I press my hands to my forehead and allow the tears to flow. "God, I'm tired. I'm so tired. More than anything, I'm afraid." I slink into the floor. "I think your word says, you haven't given us the spirit of fear, but I'm scared. Scared of failing. Scared of being back in the shape I was in fifteen years ago. Why can't I love me?"

I hit the floor with my fist.

Nobody will ever love a fat black kid.

My eyes pop open as the nightmare of the first foster home I was placed in pops into my head. The couple's name was Jo and Phil Griffin. I hated them. They would feed me less than the other children due to my size, rarely combed my hair because of the texture and told me repeatedly, nobody would ever love a fat black kid.

Hearing it enough will make you believe it.

"Help me find my strength. Help me to love me. Please God. I don't know how else to do it." I sit there with my head in my hands until my watch vibrates with a reminder of the interview. Exhaling, I look up. "I can't do this without you Lord. I've messed up. I'm messed up. Please God, I need you and I'm sorry for having you on hold so long. Have your way in my life. And God, whatever you have for me, lead me in the direction even if it means

changing everything I know. Thank you, God and amen."
I whisper before going into the bathroom to rewash my
face.

chapter seven

Fifteen minutes to eight, I give myself a pep talk and get out of the truck.

"Name please." The security guy says, never looking up.

"Ava Gentry."

"I need a photo identification and sign the clip board." He points.

I hand it to him. He taps on the computer and a few seconds later, hands me a temporary badge then points to a place I can sit. My leg is nervously shaking as I look around the atrium of the building. Inhaling and exhaling to calm myself, I grab a magazine and start to flip through it. Unsatisfied, I put it down and take out my phone. Opening Facebook, I see a friend request from Katrina.

Accepting it, I scroll down her timeline, stopping at a post from three days ago.

God doesn't reward us for being good. Truth is, most of us aren't even good on our best day. However, God rewards us because of His promise way before we were born. His promise to supply all of our needs according to His riches. Promises of plans for our life, peace, hope, health, freedom, and prosperity. For the Bible tells us in *Second Corinthians 1:20, "For all of God's promises have been fulfilled in Christ with a resounding "Yes!" And through Christ, our "Amen" (which means "Yes") ascends to God for his glory.""* I just thought I'd remind somebody today. God's promise is still yours. All He needs is a yes from you. Don't worry about what you've been through, what you're currently facing or even about tomorrow. Give God your yes and see if He won't deliver, on time, every time. I love y'all.

Someone touches my arm. "Are you Ava?"

"Yes, and I apologize."

"Hi, I'm Sharon. Please follow me."

She shows me inside an office where she hands me an iPad and a small piece of paper.

"It should take you about thirty minutes to complete the assessment. This is your login and password. I'll be back. If you have any problems, open the door and my assistant can help you."

"Thank you."

Sitting my things on the table, I take a seat at the desk, pressing the button to open the iPad and enter login information into an app call Onboarding. In exactly thirty minutes she's opening the door.

"Are you done?"

"I am."

She takes the tablet and sits across from me.

"As I stated before, my name is Sharon and I'm the Human Resource Director for Ruthie and Associates. We're a medical device company specializing in all facets of the industry. As a Senior Executive, you'll work with our acquisition department seeking out businesses, early in their life cycle, we feel will become a significant asset to the industry down the line. I see you were a project manager with Paxton and Associates. Can you tell me why you're no longer there?"

"The company was taken over by the owner's son who wanted a fresh set of employees."

"And you worked there for—

"Thirteen years."

"How did you hear about this position?"

"It came across my LinkedIn feed." I answer.

She nods, making notes. "In the job description, it mentioned traveling as we have clients all over the world. Do you own a passport and is it up to date?"

"Yes."

"Good. As an executive for Ruthie and Associates, your responsibilities will include drafting and completing contracts for new, existing, and returning clients. There are no standard set of hours for this position as you may need to attend after hour meetings and occasionally make visits to a client's location, if necessary. Is that something you're okay with?"

"Yes."

"If hired, you'll shadow one of our executives for a week as you get accustomed to the job. Do you have any questions?"

"What about benefits?" I inquire.

"We offer a benefit package that begin on your first day of employment. It also includes two weeks of vacation, two personal days and two weeks of sick time."

"Sounds good."

"Do you think this is something you can handle?"

"I'm going to surely give it my full effort."

"Great. If there are no more questions, follow me."

I move to catch up with her as she leads me inside double doors.

Stopping, I take a step back. "This is a lab. You aren't implanting some kind of chip into me, are you? I've seen Squid Games."

She laughs. "No. I can assure you this isn't the case. This is where you'll do your drug test."

"Whew, okay. Thanks Sharon."

"Name please."

"Oh God." I jump from the woman who scared me stiff. "I wasn't expecting you to be there."

"Name please."

"Ava Gentry."

"Verify your date of birth and last four of your social."

"11/19/1983 and 8767."

"Here." She shoves a cup into my hands and points to a door. "When you're done, sit this inside the metal box on the wall. Do not flush the toilet, but please wash your hands. Any questions?"

"Nope."

It takes a few minutes, but I'm finally able to fill the cup. Outside the door, Gertrude which may not be her name, but it fits her attitude is standing guard. "You're all done."

"Thanks."

Leaving the lab, I see Sharon.

"Ava, we will have the results of your test within a few days. If everything goes well, and you're selected, you'll receive an email with further instructions."

"Thanks and it was nice meeting you."

Walking to the truck with a smile feeling like things are looking up until I see the flat tire. "Freaking great."

Opening the trunk, I look for the cordless impact drill I purchased to remove lug nuts. Searching, it's not there.

Taking out my phone, I dial Andre's number. He ignores the call with a text response.

Mistake: Busy

Me: I have a flat. Did you move my drill?

Mistake: Maybe, I don't know.

Me: Why would you touch my stuff? Now, I'm stuck.

Mistake: Quit tripping and call Triple A.

Me: finger sign emoji

Tapping the Map App to search for the nearest tire shop, I see one four miles away. Closing the trunk and getting inside, I drop the phone in my lap. The only way I'll know if I can make it is to try.

"We shall see." I mumble starting the truck.

chapter eight

Pressing reverse, the truck signals to a car being behind me. I jump from a knock on the window. I hit the button to let it down.

"Didn't mean to startle you, but your left back tire is on flat."

"Thank you. I'm headed to a nearby tire shop because I don't have the tools to change it."

"You change tires?"

"What is that supposed to mean? Yes, I'm capable of changing a flat or did you think I'm too fat? Typical. Well, I'll have you know I'm more than capable." I start to let the window up.

"Wait. I didn't mean to insinuate your inability to change a tire. I only meant because you're a beautiful woman and shouldn't have too. I apologize if I made you think otherwise."

"Yeah, okay. Thanks for letting me know."

"Ma'am, you're not going to make it. If you have a spare, I can do it for you."

"You change tires?" I mockingly ask and he laughs.

"I've been known to change one or two."

"Who would have thought with your pressed white shirt and tie."

"Don't let the smooth taste fool you. Pop your trunk."

He walks away and I sigh, putting my truck in park, hitting the trunk release, and turning off the ignition. I get out and join him.

"What can I do to help?"

"You can sit in my car to stay warm if you'd like. I'm Haden by the way."

"Ava, and I apologize for the attitude. My future ex took the drill I use to remove the lug nuts and it carried over to you."

"I get it."

I step away to let him pass and watch him as he changes the tire with very little effort. When he's done, I pull some hand wipes from the kit, giving them to him once he places the old tire in the trunk.

"Thanks. Your spare could use a little air too, but it should allow you to get to the tire shop. I believe there's one not far from here."

"There is and I'm headed there now. Haden, thank you and again, I apologize for my attitude earlier."

"It's no problem and I'm glad I could help." He smiles.

"You can give me those." I refer to the dirty hand wipes. "Thanks again." I say for the fifth time breaking eye contact with him.

"Oh shoot," he says looking at his watch. "I'm late. Ava, it was nice meeting you. Drive safe and get that tire fix."

He jumps in his car, and I do the same.

After getting the tire replaced, I stop by an apartment complex downtown. Finishing the tour, I decide to apply. I tell him about being laid off and he assures me it shouldn't be a problem.

"Upon approval, how quickly would you like to move?" the gentleman asks.

"Is the same day too soon?" I joke. "Seriously, I'm not tied to a place now, so the first available will be perfect."

"I should have everything done within a week. How about March eighth?"

"That works."

"Great. I'll be in touch."

I walk out silently praying for all to go well. Inside the truck, I look at my watch, deciding to go by Lottie's. Pulling up, I see a few cars in the parking lot. At the door, I pull on it and it's locked. Peeping inside, I knock.

A young lady comes over. "Ma'am, we're not open yet."

"I know, but I was wondering if Chuck or Marcia is here."

"Who may I say is asking?" she looks me up and down.

"Ava."

"Hold on."

I pull my jacket around me after she closes the door instead of letting me in. Minutes later, Chuck appears.

"Ava, hey. Please come in."

"Hey, I'm sorry for bothering you, but I wanted to come and apologize to you and your wife in person. Is she here?"

"You don't have to do that." He tells me. "And no, she sees patients on Monday."

"Patients?"

"She's a therapist."

"I should have known with the way she read me up and down." I chuckle. "She was right too."

"Yeah, she's been known to do that and it's definitely her calling."

"I won't hold you, but the other night I was ungrateful and out of line. You all were the walking billboard of humanity, and I threw it in your face. I'm sorry. Will you please let your wife know?"

"I will or you can tell her yourself. Here's her card."

"Chuck, you wouldn't be trying to imply I need therapy, would you?"

"Oh no, God no." He stammers.

"I'm kidding. I definitely do."

"Well, if you're ever in the area and want to stop in, you're welcome. Take care Ava."

"You as well."

The following Sunday, I get up and dress for church. Coming out of the guestroom, Andre is sitting in the kitchen.

He jumps up when I walk in. "Good, you're up. We need to talk."

"Good morning to you too. What's up?"

"I have the papers here for my motorcycle. I need you to sign them before the sale ends today."

"No."

"What did you say?"

"I said no."

"Why not? Are you still upset about Tan? Come on Ava, we aren't exclusive."

"I'm not upset about Tan. However, a. I don't have a job. B. I'm not being responsible for something else we both know you aren't going to pay for. C. Because I can say no."

"Then D, you gotta go."

I shake my head. "Okay. I'm in the process of finding somewhere anyway."

"No, I mean today."

"Really Andre. You're kicking me out?"

"I am. If you're no benefit to me, why have you here? Like you said, you have no job which means no money coming in. You aren't putting out and you haven't cooked in over a week. So, yeah you gats to roll big momma. I ain't in the business of taking care of strays."

"Now I'm a stray? Wow."

"Stray, mut, orphan—whatever you choose to call yourself other than my problem."

"Nigga, I ain't never been your problem because I've always taken care of myself and you since we're being honest. This house was falling apart until I fixed it. Your credit couldn't get a free pencil from the library, until me. When your grandmother died and you were crying like a baby and talking about killing yourself, I was there."

"Cue the violins." He waves his hands. "Mane, save all that. You did what you were supposed to do because you owed me."

"Owed you for what?"

"For saving you."

"You didn't save me. You were the one who pursued me after getting my contact information from the police report. You found me and made promises, you never intended on keeping. You knew I was naïve, scared, broken and a child you took advantage of."

"Child? You were twenty-four."

"And you were thirty-two. Too old to be with me."

"It didn't stop you from choosing to come home with me though. All it took was a few meals at a fancy restaurant, promises and good sex to get you hooked."

"I had no one else." I scream. "Yes, I sold part of my soul to the devil, but it was better than my alternative. So you are doggone right, I chose you. Do I regret it? Sometimes. However, this time I'm choosing me. I'll be out of your house by this afternoon. Oh, the sex ain't never been good, it was all I had."

Changing out of my dress, I put on leggings, sweater and Ugg boots before heading to Walmart for totes and garbage bags. Getting back to Andre's house, I hit the brakes when I see all of my stuff thrown on the lawn. Throwing the truck in park, I get out when I see him standing in the door.

"You low down dog. You'd do all this the first time I tell you no. Throwing my stuff out, really."

"I gave you a chance to move."

"It's been an hour bastard." I yell.

"Then you should have acted faster."

"Don't do this. Move and allow me to get what I can. Please."

"Five minutes." He looks at his watch. "Go."

I get a tote from the truck, rushing inside to find the guestroom in disarray. Searching through the few clothes left, I can't find my computer nor chargers. Walking into the bathroom, I see them along with all of my makeup and toiletries in the tub covered with water.

I kneel beside it, crying.

"Um, you have three minutes buttercup." Andre laughs.

"Why would you do this? I've never done anything to you. Why Dre?"

"Because I could." He flatly states walking away.

I go over to the closet, reaching on the top shelf, breathing a sigh of relief when my fingers touch the lock box with the few personal documents I own. I put it under my arm, give one last glance at the room and walk out without a destination in mind. After driving around for about an hour, I decide on an Extended Stay. Checking in and paying for the week, I drag myself inside. Finally locking the door and dropping my purse on the bed, I stand there.

"This can't be all there is to my life. Lord, what is happening? I ain't been the best, all my life, but is this what I deserve? What more do I have to suffer through, huh? Haven't I gone through enough?"

I fall back on the bed, closing my eyes as memories of my past replay.

chapter nine

When I turned eighteen, I went back to my grandfather's house. He'd had a stroke and was being cared for by his sister who was eager to tell me all the family business. She told me my biological mom was seventeen when she had me, the product of a gang rape she suffered at a sorority party on a college campus. Never fully dealing with the trauma due to being raised in a generation who said, "keep family business in the house," she turned to drugs. Her addiction was so bad, she'd overdose by the time I turned two, leaving me in the care of my grandparents. Things were good until my grandmother drank herself to an early grave from grief of losing her only daughter when I was six.

Then it was just me and my grandfather Bernard Benjamin Gentry, I called him BB. I loved that man. He'd spend hours telling me stories of his past, showing me how to be strong and telling me how beautiful I was. Weeks after grandmother's funeral, he changed. He began to blame me for all he was suffering through. The nights he used to spend telling me stories were replaced by angry words and punches to my thighs. Even simple things like asking for juice would cause him to stand me in a corner for hours. If I cried from hunger, he'd lock me in a closet. Had it not been for a teacher noticing bruises when I was eight, he probably would have killed me.

All of this including pictures were in my file from child protective services. By my seventeenth birthday, I'd had over twelve foster parents, none worthy of calling home. During my junior year of high school, I met Jack. Jackson King. He and I were total opposites. He was white, I'm black. He was rich, I was poor. He went to the fancy private school while I was in public school. Our friends didn't hang together, and we rarely crossed paths. Yet, every day at 4:45 PM, he'd come into the grocery store where I worked after school.

Eventually, he'd be outside when I got off with a single rose, walking me the two blocks to my foster parent's house. I fell in love, and I mean hard. We'd sneak into this abandon house, on Wednesdays, for our weekly picnic where he took my virginity and we made plans for the future. Including running away together the night of our high school graduation. He was going to slip out from his party and meet me at the bus station at 9:25 PM to catch the 9:50 bus to Memphis. That night, I packed my best outfits and underwear, two pair of shoes and the two hundred twenty-seven dollars I had saved and set out for my new future.

He never showed.

The next day, he was gone, his number disconnected, and I never heard from him again. Weeks later, I boarded that bus to Memphis six weeks pregnant with a full scholarship to Rust College. Two weeks later, I'd miscarry in the shower of my dorm. By this time, I was numb to loss and pain. So, I cleaned myself up physically and closed my heart to anyone else. I worked odd jobs to make it to graduation and afterwards, it would take six months to find a job that wasn't waitressing or fast food at Paxton Logistics, a trucking and transportation company, in housekeeping then their mail room.

At twenty-three, all I could afford was a room in a rooming house on South Parkway. The neighborhood wasn't bad, although I can't say the same about the renters. It's also where I met Andre. He was one of the police officers who showed up the night I was almost killed. A night I try hard to forget.

A sound wakes me from my sleep. I sit up in the bed as voices outside get angrier and closer to my door.

"Who stole my shit? I'll kill everybody in this motherfucker if somebody don't start talking."

"Man, ain't nobody took nothing from you. You probably sold it for drugs."

"Who you talking to? Do you think I'm playing? Okay, alright. Watch this."

It gets quiet before two gunshots ring out.

"Oh my God." I gasp jumping up from the bed. A few minutes later, my door is kicked in. Junior is standing there with a wild look in his eyes and a gun in his hand.

"Junior, what are you doing?"

"I'm going to teach you bitches a lesson about stealing from me."

He raises the gun.

"I haven't stolen anything from you. Please. You don't have to do this."

"Shut up. You're either going to pay me with your body or blood."

He walks closer, putting his free hand around my neck and pushing me on the bed. Laying the gun beside my head, he unzips his pants.

"Junior, please don't do this." I cry.

He covers my mouth preparing to enter me, but the sound of sirens stops him. Quickly grabbing the gun, he puts it in my face and clicks it, but it jams. Cursing, he hits me in the mouth knocking out a few of my teeth and cracking my jaw.

"If you snitch, I'll kill you."

I rub my hand across the scar that's still there because I couldn't afford proper health care or to miss too many days from work. So, I showed up every day with my mouth wired shut and in unbearable pain. It took six years of hard work and going to school at night for my Masters, before finally getting a position in the field of Project Management as an Associate Analyst. By the time I was laid off, I'd worked my way up to Sr. Project Manager.

"Now, I'm starting over." I sit up with tears forming in my eyes. "This time won't be like the last, I can guarantee. I refuse to put me in the hands of someone who finds pleasure in breaking me." I tell myself.

You have some blame too.

I hear within the confines of my heart.

"I know that." I scold myself. "I have blame in some of this, but so do you God." I angrily hit the bed and two bugs come racing out from behind the nightstand like I disturbed them. I jump up.

"Nope. Can't do this."

Two hours later, I walk into a room at Hilton. Once the door closes, I press my back against it. My phone vibrates in my hand. I raise it to see a text from Andre's mother.

Mistake's Mammy: Glad to know my son finally kicked you to the curb. You've leeched for thirteen years and now your time is up. Good riddance.

Me: Lady, with no respect at all … f you and dude. He doesn't have anything to leech from. His penis and bank account are both small. 😰 #blocked

"You are a liar Satan with your bald face tail. You are a liar."

chapter ten

A few days later, I've purchased a new computer from Best Buy, clothes from a few stores and things to get me by while waiting to hear from the apartments I applied for. My phone's email notification sounds. Picking it up, I refresh my email and see one from Sharon.

"Ava,

Congratulations on being selected to the position of Senior Executive with Ruthie and Associates. Your official start date will be March 15, 2021, at 8 AM. On that morning, please prepare to take a photo and attend a half day orientation. You'll receive a separate email with your offer letter to include salary and benefit details. Steps will be included on how to accept or decline. If you should have any questions, reply to this email otherwise, I'll see you then.

"Yes." I scream dancing around the room. "Thank you, God. This calls for a celebratory lunch." With an extra pep in my step, I dress. Opening the door, the air catches in my throat at the sight of Andre.

"Andre, how did you know I was here?"

"I'm the police." He says pushing his way in.

"You stink." I pinch my nose. "When was the last time you had a shower?"

He ignores me, moving around the room grabbing my stuff. I snatch my clothes from him.

"What are you doing?"

"Taking you back where you belong. You haven't been answering my calls or replying to texts so, here I am. Get your stuff and let's go home." He barks.

I laugh. "Home? The place you threw me out of not even a week ago after destroying all my stuff. Um, no thanks. I'd rather be homeless."

"Cut the dramatics. You seemed to have landed on your feet. So, no harm no foul. Let's go."

"Whatever you were drinking has clearly made you delusional if you think I'm going anywhere with you. Sir, you'll never get the chance to throw me out or treat me like that again."

"Okay, I'm sorry. Is that what you want to hear? I'm sorry, but it's had its perks. Now, you know you're stronger than you realize."

I let out a hearty laugh. "Negro, that doesn't help your case."

"Oh, right. Well, scratch the last sentence."

"I'll do you one even better. How about we scratch this entire conversation because the fact remains, you threw me out the first time I stood up for myself and told you no."

"No, I gave you a choice and you chose the wrong one, but I forgive you."

"You forgive me for what exactly?"

"Thinking you had a life without me." He walks close enough to feel his breath. "You're mine."

"Dude," I gag, "oh my God. Your breath stinks and apparently, its clouding your brain because I'm not property and I for sure don't belong to you. You only want me to come back to sign for that stupid motorcycle, putting myself in debt, *again*." I emphasize pushing him away. "And for what, a place to stay? No, thanks. The last thirteen years—

"Waah, waah, waah. Spare me the emotional stroll down memory lane Ava, please." He drags out. "The last thirteen years gave you everything you wanted and allowed."

"You're right." I yell. "Yes, I did this, and I solely take the blame, but I'm no longer taking you. This time I'm choosing me."

He slowly claps. "Wow, those three nights you attended church has made you a changed woman. Thank you, Jesus." He exclaims throwing his hands in the air.

"Ava Gentry has seen the light. Hallelujah." He pretends to shout.

"Andre, get out of my room."

He laughs walking to the door. "I'm giving you until Friday, seeing it's how long you've paid for this room then I'll be back."

"Uh." I silently scream throwing the shirt I'm still holding in my hand.

After he leaves, I sit on the side of the bed.

"Why do I let him get in my head?"

Grabbing my phone, the card from Chuck falls from the nightstand.

Marcia Green, LCSW

Specializing in psychotherapy services and mental wellness support.

I dial the number.

"Yes, I'd like to make an appointment with Mrs. Green. No ma'am. Ava Gentry. Yes, as soon as possible. I need mental wellness support. Tomorrow works. No, can you give me the address?" I put the phone on speaker, opening the notepad.

"We're located at 7688 Lowell Cove in Memphis. Please arrive at least fifteen minutes early to fill out paperwork and be prepared to pay a 30 percent copay. If you have any questions before then, give us a call."

"Thanks."

Hanging up from her, I dial the number to the apartments I applied for.

"Yes ma'am, my name is Ava Gentry and I'm following up on the status of my application. Sure." She puts me on hold, and I press the speaker button. "Please God."

"Are you there?" she asks.

"Yes."

"Ms. Gentry, unfortunately we cannot approve your application at this time."

"May I ask why not?"

"We cannot verify your employment and in order to qualify, you have to make three times the rent."

"I told the young man I was recently laid off, but I start a new job on the 15th, and I can pay the rent up for six months." I explain.

"I understand and you can reapply once you're able to provide income for at least three pay periods."

"Ma'am, I need somewhere to live now."

"I'm sorry, but we have to abide by the rules set by management regarding income." She tells me.

"I get that, but is there someone else I can speak too?"

"You can leave a message for the resident manager, but she's going to tell you the same thing. What's your call back number? Hello. Would you like to leave a message?"

I end the call and sit there, frozen until my phone vibrates. Looking through tears, I see a text from Katrina.

Katrina: Hey, I pray all is well with you. Just checking to see if you'd like to join me for Bible study tonight at 6:30.

Me: Hey! I don't know if I'll be able too. However, if things change, I'll text.

Katrina: No problem. If there's anything you need, call.

Falling back on the bed, I lay the phone on my chest before abruptly sitting up.

"No Ava. No! You will not prove him right. Get your butt up and find somewhere to live." I chastise myself standing up.

chapter eleven

Hours later, I'm driving around after stopping at a few apartment complexes and getting the same response.

I'm sorry, you'll need proof of income before we can approve your application.

Turning down a side street, I pull over because tears are blurring my vision and lean my head against the headrest. "It won't always be like this, will it? God, will it?" A sob erupts so heavy, I have to press the button to put the truck in park and open the door, starting to feel sick. After dry heaving, I close the door and begin hitting the steering wheel.

Minutes later, I jump when my door opens. I look over and see a police officer and it makes me cry harder.

"Ma'am, are you okay?" I hear him say, but I can't answer. "Ma'am, do you need medical attention?"

"It won't always be like this, will it?"

"What's that?" he inquires.

"Life."

"Ma'am, are you in trouble?"

I shake my head no.

"Do you need EMS?"

I shake my head no, again.

"Are you sure? You aren't thinking of hurting yourself, are you?"

"I'm sorry." I whisper in between sobs. "Just having a moment."

"It's okay to have a moment as long as you allow it to end with the moment, and you begin again."

"It's hard." I cry patting my chest. "So hard."

"Okay, listen to me. Breathe. Take a breath." He coaches.

I lean forward following his instructions.

"Good. You're okay."

"I'm sorry." I tell him after the few minutes it takes to calm down.

"Don't apologize for needing to cry. Sometimes you have to cry while going through your crisis simply to survive. The good news, your tears are watering the seeds of survival and soon enough you'll be able to reap from your harvest. Do you believe in God?"

I nod, yes. "I don't think He believes in me though."

He laughs. "That's your emotions talking. Hi, I'm Josiah Rainey."

"Ava."

"Ava, here's what I love about God. You can take Him at His word, believing He'll do everything He promises even if you don't see it yet. Will you trust that God hasn't forgotten you?"

I nod yes, again.

"Good. Now, what has you on the side of the street beating the mess out of this steering wheel?"

"I'm so embarrassed." I cover my face. "Oh my God, are you going to arrest me?"

"No ma'am. Well, unless the steering wheel wants to press charges, or the truck is stolen."

"It's not, I promise, and I think the steering wheel will decline."

"I'm kidding. I'm not even on shift yet. I was headed in when I saw you and it looked like you needed help. Do you need help Ava?"

"It's been a rough couple of weeks." I admit. "I've been out looking for a place to rent, but I recently lost my job, and nobody will approve me without proof of income. It doesn't matter I'm starting a new job or have money to pay rent for a few months, I need proof. And I'm in a freaking hotel because the guy I was in an entrapment with put me out. I know you may think I'm crazy, I'm not. Although, I did book an appointment with a therapist to get my life together, but she can't see me until tomorrow. Man, it feels like my life is falling apart."

"Wow. You said all of that without taking a breath." He laughs. "And entrapment. Don't you mean entanglement?"

"No, it was very much a trap. Anyway, sorry for blabbering, I know you have to get to work. I'm okay now and I won't inflict anymore harm on the steering wheel. Thank you for stopping."

"Be safe Ava and believe God." He turns to leave then stop. "I hardly ever come this way when headed to work." He blurts. "I thought God was protecting me from an accident or something."

It's my turn to look at him.

"Now, I'm the one blabbering. Ava, do you believe God put people in specific places to handle assignments we wouldn't see otherwise?"

"I guess so, but I've only recently taken God off hold so what do I know." I shrug.

He looks confused.

"It's a long story."

"Oh. Well, this is going to sound weird or farfetched, whichever way you take it. However, I happen to have a 2-bedroom townhouse that'll be available next Friday. It's nothing fancy—

"I'll take it." I interrupt.

"Wait." He laughs. "You haven't seen it or heard any of the details."

"Is it in a safe part of town with doors that lock, a roof, no insect infestation and able to get utilities?"

"Yes."

"How much is the rent?"

"850 with one month security deposit."

"I don't have a job currently, but I start one on the 15th and I can pay a few months of rent up front."

"I remember."

"I can also pass a background check and have no evictions on my credit." I hurriedly tell him before he changes his mind.

"Cool. Can you meet me tomorrow afternoon around three to see it and fill out the application?"

"Perfect, no wait. I have an appointment with a new therapist. Can we do it before or after?"

"Um, my wife can possibly meet you. Let me call her."

He walks away.

"Okay God, please let this be you and not some serial killer, stalker type stuff."

He comes back, handing me his phone.

"Ava, this is my wife, Naomi."

"Oh, uh, hi." I say looking at her via Facetime.

"Hey," she says after swallowing. "My apologies, I didn't realize my husband would rudely shove his phone in your face while I'm eating lunch. Men. Hi Ava. I can't meet you tomorrow, but I can set it up for you to tour it on your own today, if possible. Also, there are applications on the kitchen counter and if interested, you can complete it then stop by my office and drop it off. Does that work for you?"

"It does."

"Cool. Give my husband your contact information and I'll shoot a code to the lockbox via text along with the address."

"Thank you, Naomi."

I hand him the phone back.

"Babe, I have to go. Love you." She tells him.

"This doesn't seem real." I say out loud.

"An unexpected blessing never seems real. Yet, you must trust God, remember. What's your full name, number and can I take a picture of your identification for security reasons?"

I rattle it off, hand him my license and a few minutes later, my phone vibrates.

"I sent you the address. I'll also send your number and picture to Naomi. Here's my wife's card. If you have any questions, call. It was nice meeting you Ava. Oh, God says, no it won't always be like this, yet sometimes we have to suffer in order to surrender self to God. It's in our surrendering we remove the opposition between us and God's plans for our life. Hmm, that'll preach." He laughs. "Be safe."

He closes the door and walks away. When he passes in his squad car, I wave.

"God, I thank you and trust what you're doing even if I don't understand it or see it yet."

chapter twelve

I'm walking through the townhouse wearing a huge smile while praying, Lord, let this be it. Once done, I sit in my car filling out the application before stopping to get a money order and heading to Visions, a portrait studio.

"Welcome to Visions, do you have an appointment?" the young lady asks.

"Hey, no, I'm here to see Naomi. My name is Ava Gentry."

"One moment." She comes back. "You can follow me."

She points me inside the office door.

"Ava, hi, I'm Naomi. It's nice to officially meet you. Please have a seat. How did you like the townhouse?"

"I love it. Here's the application with a money order for the $25 application fee."

"Thank you. I forgot to mention it when we spoke."

"No worries. I'm just appreciative to you and your husband. I had no idea what I was going to do and when he found me, I was a mess. I'm sure he told you."

"He didn't. I assumed it was a traffic stop. He's been known to give my information with tickets." She laughs. "Can't say I'm upset because it increases business."

"I wish it was a ticket."

"Girl, who wishes for a ticket?"

"Let's just say I'd had a bad morning, well more like a bad month, and took it out on my steering wheel. I was in full breakdown mode with crying and screaming that I didn't even notice he'd pulled up and opened my door. He must have thought I was losing my mind. It was so embarrassing."

"Honey, we've all been there and sometimes it helps to get it out. I'd much rather it be the steering wheel than your life."

"Yeah, but I seem to be there a lot lately and hoping things will soon turn in my favor."

"They will if you believe. Here's what I love about God."

"You sound like your husband. He said the same thing."

She chuckles. "We do love us some God because He has been there for us more than He should. Ava, it's easy to look at us and think we have our life together, but it wasn't always like this. We've known our fair share of struggle. Nonetheless, what I love about the God we serve, He'll allow us to get struck down, but not destroyed. While I don't know what caused you to be in the shape you were and neither do I have all the answers. I can assure this, you will survive."

"I believe I will, it's just somedays I don't know how."

"By getting up and doing, especially when you don't have the strength, energy or understanding. Girl, if there's anything I've learned, it's with every new second of life, there's new seconds of hope."

"Thank you, Naomi. I'm going to take your wisdom to heart. Anyway, I won't hold you. I appreciate you and your husband. It's not every day you find someone willing to give you a chance." I stand and she does too.

"Somebody took a chance on us, many years ago, and it's one of the reasons we're in a position to return the favor to others. Ava, it was nice meeting you and once I have everything back, I'll give you a call. Should take a few days."

"Thank you and please let your husband know, I'm truly grateful for what he did. He wasn't on duty, yet he still stopped to make sure I was okay. I'll never forget his kindness."

"That's my Josiah. I'll be sure to tell him."

Getting back to the hotel, I stop by the front desk to extend my stay for another week. Later in the evening, after a shower I dress and walk across the street to Benihana.

After being seated at the bar, I order a Benihana punch, spicy chicken rice and chili shrimp sushi. Taking my phone from my purse, I see the texts and calls from Andre.

Mistake: You're being childish Ava.

Mistake: Answer my calls

Mistake: I'm sorry okay. What else do you want me to say?

Mistake: Fine! Ignore me. We'll see who will have the last laugh.

I block him and prepare to enjoy my night.

The next afternoon, I nervously wait for my session with Dr. Greene.

"Ava, hey, it's nice to see you again." Marcia greets coming in.

I stand. "Hey. At least it's not 2 AM in the back of your bar. I'm sorry about that, by the way."

"Apology accepted. Please have a seat and tell me a little about yourself."

I exhale. "Well, there's not much to tell. I'm 37 years old, never been married, no children, raised in foster care from the time I was eight and been in a situation-ship with an older man who has never loved me, but thinks he saved me."

"Is that what you think? Did he save you?"

I pause. "In a way, yes yet not to his magnitude of thinking. I was twenty-four, living in a rooming house and working in housekeeping trying to land a decent job. One night I was attacked, and he was an officer who showed up. A week later, he called and invited me out to dinner. That night, I had too much to drink and went home with him. The rest is miserable history."

"Yet, you stayed. Why?"

"I don't know."

"Sure you do." She states. "Even when we don't want to admit the why, we certainly know it."

"He was all I had." I admit. "He gave me a place to stay and for the first time, I felt safe and, in a way, loved. Well, what I thought was love. We'd go out on dates, he showered me with gifts, gave me a place to live and he was the first to ever celebrate my birthday."

"In other words, he appealed to everything you'd been missing."

"Yeah, and he was great at it. Until he wasn't."

"Why did he stop?" she questions.

"Because I didn't hold him accountable, and he didn't press the issue because he was getting what he wanted. He told me, he was only doing what I required and allowed. Sad reality, he's right."

"Why do you think that is?"

"I guess, a small part of me didn't think I was worthy of anything more. Don't get me wrong, Andre had the potential to be a good partner, but he can also act like a child needing to be taken care of."

"Ava, we could spend the remaining of your session talking about your relationship and all the things wrong with him, but this isn't about him. What do you need?"

"I need me." I reply, choking up.

"Then let's find Ava."

"There's the problem. I don't know who she is or where to find her. I am just a girl, born to a teenage mother in Dothan, Alabama after being conceived during a gang rape who died when I was two. Then I was raised by my grandparents. My grandmother would only let me call her Pearl because she blamed me for the death of her only child until she drank herself to an early death. Then my grandfather changed into a physically abusive monster and terrorized me till I was taken away at eight. Let's not even talk about the foster system. I don't know who the hell I am, Dr. Greene. Sometimes I think it would have been better if my mother would have killed me instead. Dying has to be better than this."

"Then do it."

"Do what?" I question wiping my face.

"Kill yourself."

chapter thirteen

Dr. Marcia Greene

"Wait, what?"

"Kill yourself." I repeat.

"I, um, I, you've lost your mind lady." She stands frantically grabbing her purse. "I know I kissed your husband and you're probably still a little salty about it, but to suggest I kill myself is the most asinine thing I've heard. And I've heard some pretty crazy stuff lately." She gets to the door and stops. "I want to live. No, I am going to live and if I was suicidal, coming here wouldn't have helped. Thanks, but no."

"Ava, wait."

"Hell no. You must have gotten your degree from an institution who needed black chicks to keep funding because I know, nobody certified you telling someone to kill themselves. And you got the nerve to say it with a straight face. Girl, forget you and I'm reporting you to the state of whomever gave you a license."

"Ava, please hear me out. Please." I point to the couch. She turns back, folding her arms.

"When I say kill yourself, I don't mean you personally. I mean Y-O-U-R space S-E-L-F as in flesh. See, when you're in self, the suffering you endure becomes personal. You'll believe it's punishment from God which leads you to denying or even hating God and life. Self doesn't let you see past pain. Self doesn't allow you to believe things won't always be like this. Self says you deserve a man who'll belittle you because you're not worthy of being someone's good thing from God. Self makes you believe the narrative your granddaddy drilled into your head. Self will never allow you to be free. Staying in self will never let you see beyond now, and this is why it'll be hard for you to identify who you are."

"Then why not lead with this?"

"Because it made you angry enough to fight for your life and it's going to be this anger that'll help you make it through the process of dying to self. Ava, the next phase of your life is going to be one of the hardest."

"Nothing can be harder than what I've gone through."

"This will because you'll have to face things you've filed away, secrets you longed forgotten about and a past that didn't treat you well. What you've gone through is things you survived but dying to self is surviving you and sometimes that means taking a hard look at everything about you. In doing so, the veil is pulled back and you might not like the truths you'll have to admit."

"If it gets me beyond this darkness, where do I begin?" I ask retaking my seat.

"Do you believe in God?"

"Yes."

"Then start with fasting. Fasting is self-sacrifice where one chooses to abstain from food, replacing it with prayer, reading God's word or simply spending alone time with Him. Fasting allows God to purify us, spiritually while detoxing physically. Fasting isn't something to play with because God can utilize periods of fasting to show us our true self, especially the ugly parts we don't want to see. I will not lie, it's going to take patience, strength, willingness and your determination to make it through."

"How long should I fast?"

"I suggest starting for three days, 6 AM to 6 PM drinking nothing but water. While you fast, pray because things may get hectic in your life, and it'll make you want to give up. Don't. The enemy will tempt you, don't fall for it and if you mess up, start again. Also, write down things that'll seem abnormal or weird, like your dreams and make a list of things you want God to do for you and pray on them." I get up and get my phone, searching through the Bible App. "Bible says in Second Timothy two, verses eleven through thirteen, *"This is a trustworthy saying. If we die with him, we will also live with him. If we endure hardship, we will reign with him. If we deny him, he will deny us. If we are unfaithful, he remains faithful, for he cannot deny who he is.""*

"What does the last part mean?" I ask.

"No matter what we do or how unfaithful we are to God, He'll always remain faithful, committed, reliable and trustworthy because it's who He is. Baby, there's been plenty of times I wasn't deserving of God's grace, yet He shows up, bailing me out of trouble because it's His reputation on the line. It's like a couple I counseled once. The husband knew his wife had been unfaithful multiple times, but he never cheated. In their last session before he filed for divorce, he told her the reason he wasn't unfaithful was not due to how well she kept a house, how good she was in bed nor the way she could lie which she wasn't good at. He said it was because he wouldn't let her change who he was and risk losing everything and tainting his reputation with God and people."

"God doesn't do it because of me, He does it in spite of me." I realize.

"Yes, because He hopes along the way, you'll turn back to Him, repenting and desiring to step into the plans and purpose He's had for your life all along. Ava, you've been through a lot in your life, but you still have a lot of life left to live. You can either do so, introducing Ava as the girl whose life hasn't been easy, the end or you can add to the narrative by saying, hi, my name is Ava, and my life hasn't been easy nevertheless dot, dot, dot. Nevertheless, an adverb which means in spite of that. My life hasn't been easy, nevertheless, I'm here and I got another chance. I hope this makes sense."

"It does. It gives me a lot to think about."

"Good. Ava, thank you for making the first step in restarting your life."

"Restarting, I like that."

"Often times we think we need to start over when what we really need is a restart. When you restart a computer or phone, you're essentially resetting the system's logic by flushing the memory, wiping away whatever was happening previously and restarting in a new state. Unlike computers, we can't wipe away the memories of the past or present, but we can surely flush our system to begin again in a new state, i.e. mind frame."

"I like that. Restarting my life. Thank you, Dr. Greene. Will it be okay if I scheduled another appointment with you?"

"Of course. Can I pray with you before you go?"

"Please."

I stand and take her hands. "God of infinite grace, wisdom and love. Thank you. Thank you for this day, the things you've allowed to happen and those you've blocked. God, thank you for Ava and the steps she's taken to restart her life. Father, be there for her, not just with your presence but with provisions, protection, plans, peace, patience, people, and your power. God, you gave her the courage to press the spiritual reset button, now give her strength to continue and the patience to endure the rough parts of starting again. God, I know it won't be easy, yet do it for her. She's lived long enough without you, let her experience what life is like with you. And God, surround her with people who'll love and help her through this reconstruction phase. You know who and what she needs, meet it like only you can. In the name of Jesus, I pray. Amen."

"Amen."

"Oh Ava, for the record, I was never salty about you kissing my husband. I trust him."

"I know and I apologize for my actions."

"I understand, just don't let it happen again." I smile. "Be safe and I'll see you next time."

chapter fourteen
Ava

A week later, I stretch out on the air mattress kicking my legs, excited about spending the first night in my new home. Sitting up, I look around the empty room and begin to thank God. After a shower, change of clothes and a few offbeat dance moves through the empty townhouse, I fall back on the mattress.

"God, I'm absolutely sure I don't know what you have planned for my life, but can you give me strength and grace to get through it? Amen."

Grabbing my new Bible, notepad, and phone from the floor I begin the process of working on me. Unlocking the phone, I open Safari. "Okay Google, help a sista out." I type in 'dying to self bible verse,' and click enter making note of a few scriptures and thoughts. Flipping through the Bible, I find First Corinthians three and sixteen, reading it out loud. *"Do you not know that you are the temple of God and that the Spirit of God dwells in you?"* No, I didn't know this." I answer myself. "But I'm learning."

My stomach growls and I look at my watch, realizing a few hours have passed. Pushing the things away, I decide to take a mental health day. Walking out, I stand inside the garage with a huge smile.

"Okay Ava, you're being weird." I laugh at myself. Getting in the truck, I open the map app to search for a local spa. Reading through the reviews and checking the website, I decide on one not far.

"Good morning. Do you have an appointment?" the young lady asks.

"Good morning and no, I don't but I was hoping you'd have space to fit me in."

"No problem. Tell me what services you're interested in, and I can check."

"Um, the works."

She laughs handing me a card. "We offer massages, facials, manicures, pedicures, and waxing services. I can fit you in for a massage, manicure, pedicure, and Brazilian wax with Nedra in forty-five minutes."

"That works for me."

"Great. Fill this out and I can get you scheduled."

Three hours and some change later, I feel like a new woman.

"Hey Ava, my name is Tabitha. Is this your first time getting a wax?" the young lady questions walking into the room while I lay on a table with my who-ha on display.

"Yes. I normally do all my grooming at home."

"Understandable. No need to be nervous." She pats my leg.

"Is this going to hurt?"

"Well, it's not going to be comfortable, but it's tolerable." She comes over and stops, looking up at me. "Okay, yeah, um this is going to hurt. Please butterfly your legs."

I jump.

"This is only powder."

"Not so bad." I chuckle.

"Now, I'll begin. Please let me know if the wax is too hot."

"No, it's good."

I close my eyes trying to think of anything but what's happening below.

"One, two— she snatches the wax.

"Praise be to God. What happened to three?" I holler out raising up. "It feels like you're ripping hair from middle school. Jesus, the little bitty baby." I pant.

"Breathe. You made it through the first one."

"How many more are there?"

"A few. Here comes more wax." She warns. "If it's too hot, let me know. Okay, here we go."

"Aww, Lord-a-mercy. Forgive me for any and all sins."

She removes another strip.

"Swing low, sweet chariot. Coming for to carry me home." I begin to sing. "Jesus Christ." Humming to tune her out, I stop when I hear her say one more.

"I'm going to apply some aloe oil then I'll need you to pull your legs up to your chest."

"For what?"

"To remove the hair from your butt."

"My what? Oh no ma'am. The back door is off limits, even to God. No ma'am. Unuh girlfriend."

She laughs. "It's a part of the full wax and it's only one strip. It'll be over before you know it. However, you can choose to skip it."

"Well, since you've been places light hasn't seen in a while, go ahead."

Finally done, I throw my legs over the table.

"I feel like you owe me a cigarette."

She laughs. "It'll be better next time."

"Next time? People actually return to pay for this kind of torture?"

"Of course."

"Girl. We'll see."

Afterwards, I visit a few furniture stores ordering things I need to furnish the townhouse. Lining all of the deliveries to be around the same time, I'm well pleased with all I've accomplished. Once done, I stop by a hair salon in Walmart for a silk press. An hour later, I pay the lady and shop for a few things before heading home.

Home. I love the sound of that.

Later in the evening, sitting in the middle of the living room floor with a pizza from Papa John's, a bottle of wine and my computer watching Sweet Magnolia's on Netflix there's a knock on the door.

Pausing the show, I tiptoe over to the door. Looking out the side window, I let out an exasperated sigh.

"Andre, what are you doing here?"

"I should be asking you the same thing."

I press my hand to his chest when he tries to push his way in. "Hold up partner. How did you know where I was?"

"You aren't going to let me in?"

"No." I state moving closer to block his access.

"You got company? Whose place is this? Why aren't you letting me in? Are you squatting in these people's place? Come on Ava. This is low even for you."

"Are you done with the interrogation questions?"

"I will be if you let me in."

"Andre, it's late and I'm not about to play twenty questions with you. I don't owe you an answer, explanation, or reasoning for what I do because I'm no longer your problem. Do us both a favor and leave me alone."

I slam the door ensuring it's locked, returning to my spot when he begins to pound on it. He beats until the neighbor threatens to call the police. When he drives off, I get my phone and search, 'how do you know if there's a tracking device on your car?'

"It will typically look like a small box with a magnetic side. It may or may not have an antenna or light and it'll be small." I read, going out to the garage with my flashlight on. It takes about thirty minutes of searching inside and out, and I don't find anything.

"How else can he find where I am?" I question sitting in the passenger seat of the truck. "Phone." I sit up, opening each of the grouped apps. On the last screen, I see a Life360 app. Clicking it and my mouth falls open. I touch the settings to see he's created an email address, fatgirlAva@gmail.com.

"Bastard." I seethe while pressing to delete the account then removing the icon.

Unblocking his contact, I send a text.

Me: You dirty, rotten dog. I can't believe you've been tracking me all this time.

I start pacing talking to myself until I hear the notification.

Mistake: Don't you track your packages?

I start to type out a whole line of cuss words but decide against it and instead place him back on the block list. Taking one last glance at the remaining apps, I ensure there aren't any more I didn't install.

"Lord, please sever this tie."

chapter fifteen
Monday, March 15, 2021

"Good morning. My name is Ava Gentry and I'm a new employee."

The security lady holds up her finger to me as she continues to tap on the keyboard. A few minutes later, she looks up.

"Your name."

"Good morning. My name is Ava Gentry and I'm a new employee." I repeat with a slight annoyance.

"ID." She holds out her hand.

I hand it to her, and she prints out a temporary badge.

"Take the elevator to the fourth floor."

"Thank you and I pray your day gets better." I tell her walking off. "They must put all of their security through the same grumpy training. Well, not today, Satan. You will not steal my joy."

The elevator opens on the fourth floor.

"Ava?"

"That's me."

"Hi, I'm Penelope Henshaw. Welcome to Ruthie and Associates. You'll be shadowing me for the next week, so I hope you have comfortable shoes in that bag. Also, you'll want to tone down the colors." She refers to my green blazer.

"Um, tone down my colors? Why?"

"You can ask that question in orientation later. Follow me and I'll show you to your office."

As we walk the corridor, she points out the breakroom, executive wing, restrooms, conference rooms and coffee bar.

"There's a café on the second floor and fitness center in the basement. And here's your office. On your desk you'll find a cell phone, laptop, bag, mouse, and keys to the door and file cabinet. Feel free to decorate as you like. There's a storage area with things you can look through like chairs and pictures. To hang anything, call maintenance." She looks at her watch. "You have about forty-three minutes before the morning staff meeting. Spend the time getting acquainted with your computer because it's going to be your best friend. Lex from IT will be up—

A knock on the door stops her.

"Perfect timing. This is Lex who'll help you set up your laptop, company cell phone, and anything else you need. I'll be back to get you for the meeting."

"Wow." I state looking at the door.

"She talks fast. You'll get used to it." He laughs.

At 8:55 AM, Penelope is back at the door.

"Ready?"

"Yep. Is there anything I need to bring?"

"Generally, you'll need computer, pen and notepad. However, you won't need it for this meeting. Today is all about getting you adjusted to how things are done. If you listen to me, you'll do fine."

Lex is still working on my computer, so I grab my cell phone and notepad, following her. Inside the conference room, she introduces me to everyone in attendance. My eyes lock on Haden who waves. We take seats near the middle of the table.

"Good morning fellow humans. Happy Monday. We have a lot to cover today, I hope you've had your coffee." A man with a whole lot of energy sings bursting through the door.

"That's Roger, head of acquisitions." Penelope leans over to tell me. "He talks faster than me. Keep up."

The meeting last far longer than it should, however I'm excited to have my first assignment working with Penelope to acquire a new medical company called, Small Sticks. A startup by two young black men who've created a glucose monitoring system for children with Type 1 and 2 Diabetes. The machine is compact, small enough to fit in the palm of your hand and works with an app to track blood sugar levels. Ruthie and Associates have been in talks for weeks and according to Penelope, there's another business meeting in three weeks.

I put my things in the office and head to the coffee bar before the afternoon orientation.

"Ava, how are you liking Ruthie and Associates?" Haden asks coming to stand beside me.

"So far, so good. Thank you again for helping me with my tire. I'm usually prepared for things like that and when I wasn't, you were there."

"After you bit my head off."

"Yeah, not my finest moment." I chuckle.

"I'm only kidding. What are you having?" he asks.

"I don't know. What do you suggest?"

"Hmm. Do you mind if I order for you?"

"Sure."

"Your usual, Mr. Kingston?" the barista asks.

"Yes, two please. One for our newest employee."

"Yes sir."

"Congratulations on getting your first client." He says after placing the order.

"Thank you. Any advice for the new girl?"

"Ava, you're far from a girl." He winks. "My advice, take your time in learning the aspects of this job. Don't drive yourself crazy trying to learn it all in one day. Get to know your clients like the back of your hand and ask as many questions as needed to ensure you deliver on whatever promises made. Oh, don't take what Penelope says personally. Her bedside manners could use some tuning."

"Got it."

The young lady hands him two cups.

"This is my own special mix. I hope you enjoy it."

At my desk, I remove the top from the coffee. Sipping it, I cringe from the bitterness of the taste before pushing it away and planning to go back for another cup of something better.

Later, after the four-hour boring orientation, I make it back to the office to find my laptop and a sticky note with login information. The first thing I do is change the password before opening Google to find everything I can on Small Sticks. I'm in the middle of a yawn when Penelope taps on the door.

"Already burning the midnight oil?" she scoffs.

"Sorry." I say covering my mouth. "I was doing research on Small Sticks after the orientation."

"Oh, did you ask about the colors?" she wags her finger.

"I did and it's not an issue."

She looks shocked.

"Small Sticks seems to be a great company. Why are they thinking of selling?"

"Technically, they aren't. They are small and in need of capital to finance the manufacturing of their stick thingy to a larger market. Right now, it's only local. However when a company like Ruthie and Associates shows up, it's usually with an offer many don't refuse. It's my job to make sure they don't."

"If they do?" I ask.

"Do what?"

"Refuse."

"They won't." She states.

"If they do?" I push.

She shrugs. "Then we'll move on to the next."

"Let's say they agree to partner with Ruthie and Associates, what happens once the deal is done?"

"Honey, we don't partner. We buy to auction off to the highest bidder." She looks at her phone. "We can talk more tomorrow. Oh, staying late won't get you any brownie points."

I shake my head. A few minutes later, I close the laptop, standing to stretch and deciding to rearrange the furniture before leaving. Heading out of the office in search of the storage closet, I run into someone.

"I'm sorry—Jack?" I stumble back.

chapter sixteen

He grabs my arm to steady me and neither of us move. I blink a few times thinking I must be imagining things.

"Jack?" I stutter. "How, what are you doing here?" Then it hits me, and I step back. "Haden Kingston."

"He's my baby brother."

"Wow. Is this your family's company?"

"One of a few." He beams.

"Was I hired because of you?"

"No, I have nothing to do with hiring. I saw the name but didn't put it together until now. However, I can assure you. You're here because you met what we were looking for in an employee."

"Yeah, but now that you know, is my being here going to be a problem because I can grab my stuff and roll?"

"No."

"Great. Goodnight, Jack." I turn walking back into my office.

He follows me inside. "Ava, I don't want things to be weird between us."

"Why would they be? I haven't seen you in almost twenty years."

"I know, but I still need to apologize for the way I left things."

"No need. Whatever happened then no longer matters now."

"It does to me. I was wrong."

"That we can agree on."

"Ava, I'm sorry."

"Thanks."

"Is that all you're going to say?" he asks with a shocked tone.

"What is there to say? We met, you promised, broke said promises, left and I never heard from you again."

"Please give me a chance to explain."

I stop and lay the computer on the desk. "Dude, we both know the reason you left me standing at a bus stop was because daddy made you and anything you try to add isn't needed. In fact, you really didn't owe me an apology." I walk closer to him. "See, I've come to realize here recently, the deadbeat ass men in my life are my fault. Just like with Andre, I was the one foolish enough to be blinded by dreams you painted as daisies and rainbows. Your lies were the password to the sacred place between my legs. Dumb me, I allowed you to enter every time even when I knew, in my heart, you'd never choose me. Oh, it also didn't stop me from falling in love with you. Yeah, I was stupid. Nevertheless, you're off the hook and all is forgiven." I pat his cheek and turn away before the tears fall.

"I was 18, fresh out of high school and tied to my parents financially. I had to go with their plans for me or they would have cut me off completely. Ava, what kind of life could I have given you then?"

"You're right. Is that what you need to hear to ease your conscious? Fine. You're right. Now, will you please do what you didn't all those years ago?"

"What's that?"

"Say goodbye."

He doesn't say anything.

I chuckle walking over to get my computer, phone, and purse.

"Ava, I spent my entire life being groomed to walk in the footsteps of my father. Those same footprints included marrying a good, wholesome Christian woman—

"Don't forget white." I finish.

"They only wanted the best for me."

"No sweetie, they didn't want you with a fat black girl with no parents and stable home who was looking for a come up. I do believe those are the adjectives your dad used when describing me, aren't they?"

He sighs.

"It's cool. In the eyes of people like you, the rich, entitled, and judgmental, I'll always be that."

"You know I'm not like them," he says trying to grab my hand when I walk pass.

I snatch away.

"You are them. Goodbye Jack. Close the door when you leave."

Wired up from the conversation, I decide to hit the gym.

"Bag lady, you gon' hurt your back, dragging all them bags like that. I guess nobody ever told you, all you must hold on too. Is you, is you, is you? One day, all them bags gon' get in your way. One day, all them bags gon' get in your way. I said, one day, all them bags gon' get in your way. Pack light." I sing while walking on the elliptical.

I jump from someone touching me. Removing my Air Pod, I look at the young lady handing me a paper towel.

"Are you okay?" she asks coming closer.

"Yeah, why do you ask."

"You're crying."

"Oh." I tell her feeling embarrassed. "Yes, thank you. Listening to Erykah Badu and it has me in my feelings."

"Who?"

"Erykah—never mind, thank you."

"No problem."

I finish my workout and head home. Pulling up, I see flowers on the doorstep. I park in the garage, go through the house and to the front door.

Snatching off the card.

Ava, meet me for dinner and allow me to apologize.

No strings attached.

Buckley's, Friday 7 PM

Andre

I take the flowers around the side of the house and dump them in the garbage.

chapter seventeen

"You look great." Andre stands to greet me. "I didn't think you'd show."

"I started not too." I tell him, placing my jacket and purse in the chair. "Yet, I hope this is you finally coming to terms with us being over."

"Good evening, ma'am, may I offer you a glass of wine or maybe a lemon drop martini?" the server asks.

"No sir, just sweet tea and an order of Memphis Jam Bake."

"Yes ma'am. Sir, another beer?"

Andre nods.

"Why am I here?"

"I only wanted to talk to you and seeing you haven't been answering my calls or texts, I thought—

"You thought feeding me would do the trick?"

He sighs and I laugh.

"Well, I hope you brought your wallet because I haven't eaten all day."

"I didn't, I'm sorry."

"You didn't bring your wallet?" I clarify.

"Yes, I have my wallet. I meant bringing you here doesn't have a hidden agenda." He sits up. "Ava, I miss you and I truly apologize for how I handled things. These last few weeks without you have shown me how valuable you were to my life. I don't even know how to work the washing machine and—

"So you need me to do laundry?"

The waiter sits our drinks down.

"Are you all ready to order or would you like to wait until the appetizer arrives?"

"Oh, I'm ready. I'll take the 14-ounce ribeye, medium well with creamed spinach and loaded baked potato."

"For you, sir?"

"The same." Andre states handing him the menu as another waiter places the appetizer in the center of the table.

"I'll get this right in. If you need anything, my name is Fred."

"Can we—

I bow my head. "God, thank you for the food we're about to eat. Bless the hands that prepared it while removing all impurities, letting it be nourishment to our bodies. In Jesus' name, amen." I look up. "You were saying?"

"Can we start over?"

"This conversation? Sure."

"No, our relationship. Boo, I've made a lot of mistakes concerning you, especially the way I talked to and treated you. I took your presence for granted and now, if you'll give me the chance, I will make things right. I'll be a better man and well, here. I have something for you." He smiles.

I place the napkin in my lap and take the envelope. Opening it, I shake my head.

"A $500 gift card?"

"I know it doesn't cover everything I destroyed, but it's a start and I promise to replace your computer too."

"I've already replaced the computer but thank you." I say putting the card in my purse.

"How? I thought you didn't have money."

"No, you assumed."

We sit in silence as I finish the appetizer before pushing the plate away. "Andre, what's my favorite color?"

His brows crease. "Um, white."

"Green. What's my middle name?"

"Janice, no Jackie." He snaps his finger, excitedly.

"Justine. When is my birthday?"

"Why are you asking me all this?"

I pause while our food is put in front of us.

"Is there anything else you need?" Fred inquires.

We both nod, no.

"Enjoy."

"Because you don't know me. Andre, you don't miss me. You miss what I do for you. The cooking, cleaning, paying bills and the sex. Any other time I'm fat, ugly, uneducated, sleeping my way to the top and nobody would ever want me. Today, I'm boo. Okay." I laugh cutting into my steak. "Since we're laying everything on the table, let's be all the way real. You've never loved or hell, even liked me unless there was something in it for you. It didn't matter how much I tried or gave it was never enough. Now, I'm supposed to accept the new you who magically appeared in three weeks when you've had thirteen years? No thank you. Pass the steak sauce."

"You're right. I didn't put any effort into our relationship because, honestly, I didn't believe I had too. Ava, you never required me to show you anything else."

I chuckle. "So, it's still my fault? If I was in the hospital, unable to tell the doctors and nurses how to care for me, does that give them the right to mistreat me? As an officer of the law, should a person you've pulled over have to tell you to treat them with respect?"

"Of course not."

"Then why should I have to tell you how to treat me?" I say louder than I expected. "Andre, I get my part in this relationship, but you also have blame. Yet, even sitting here, your apology is voided by but. Ava, I'm sorry for calling you out of your name every chance I got, but you never did anything about it. Ava, I'm sorry for ruining your credit, twice, but you let me. Ava, I didn't love you, but you never said I had too."

"I'm sorry." He whispers. "This isn't going how I planned."

"Because you expected the same Ava you threw out along with everything I owned. I'm not her. Yes, we both went into this relationship with our eyes closed and expectations low, yet even when I was changing, you were staying the same. My only regret, putting more into you than you were worth. Andre, I'm not the same and you need to recognize this."

We eat in silence for the next twenty minutes.

"Ma'am, may I pack this up for you?" Fred asks referring to my leftovers.

"Please."

"Did you save room for dessert?"

"God no. I'm stuffed."

He looks at Andre. "What about you? Can I show you our dessert menu?"

"Sure."

"I'll be right back."

"Thank you for dinner and although our relationship is over, I pray God's best for you concerning your life." I grab my jacket and purse while waiting for my leftovers.

"Ava, wait."

Fred comes back with a plate, sitting it in front of me.

"I didn't— stopping when I see what's written around the edge.

Will you marry me?

Andre gets down on one knee.

"This nigga." I say under my breath, plastering on a smile.

"Ava Justine Gentry. I know it's taken me thirteen years to truly see you, but I love you and I want to spend the rest of my life showing you just how much. Will you marry me?"

"Aw." People are saying and staring.

He takes my hand pulling me into a standing position.

"Say yes girl." Someone yells.

"Yes." I whisper.

"She said yes." Fred announces as Andre slides the ring halfway up my finger.

Walking out, Andre is all smiles while fist bumping some of the men. Getting to my truck, I open the door, putting the to go bag and my things inside.

"Will you come home with me?" Andre asks.

I turn around, grabbing him by his shirt, pulling him close enough that our lips almost touch. "I wouldn't come home with you if it and the riverbank of the Mississippi were my only options to sleep. Neither am I marrying you. Negro, you don't deserve me."

"Then why say yes?"

"To spare you the embarrassment of saying no. You're welcome. Oh, and the next time you want to propose, get the ring size right." I snatch it off, pressing it to his chest. "Andre, we're over. Please move on with your life and allow me the space to do the same."

Making it home, I go over to the garbage stuffing the leftovers inside. "He really thought I'd marry him because he bought a steak and potato served with empty promises? Who does he think he is?"

I grab the bottle of wine from the refrigerator, getting frustrated when I can't get it open. Finally pulling the cork out, I take a long gulp. "Am I that gullible or maybe he thinks I'm pathetic enough to say yes. Raggedy, Chester the homeless alley cat looking winch. Ava Justine Gentry, will you marry me?" I mock. "Nigga, I wouldn't marry you if your insurance could give me the heart transplant I needed to live."

I take another swig of wine, sitting it on the nightstand, stripping out of my clothes and standing in front of the full-length mirror.

"He doesn't deserve you. You're beautiful. You're smart. You're worthy." I walk closer. "Who am I kidding?" I question my reflection, rubbing the scars on my thighs from the abuse I suffered as a child. "I'm broken."

The next morning, I'm jolted awake by someone hammering outside. I look down realizing I only have on underwear, and I fell asleep on top of the air mattress that's now flat. Rising, I groan seeing the empty wine bottle beside me and from the pain. Falling onto my back, I stare at the ceiling as tears fall.

My phone continually vibrates.

(901) 234-0098: Ava, it's Andre. Please unblock my number and talk to me.

(901) 234-0098: Will you at least think about the proposal?

(901) 234-0098: I'm sorry okay. This isn't all on me.

(901) 234-0098: Give me one more chance.

(901) 234-0098: You should be happy I asked you.

(901) 234-0098: I'll leave you alone because I don't beg. Good riddance.

Without replying, I block this number too.

chapter eighteen

A week or so later, June and I are sprawled out on my living room floor laughing about Andre's proposal over margaritas. All of my furniture has been delivered and although I haven't finished decorating, I wanted her to see it.

"Girl, you should have left him on his knee and walked out with your leftovers."

"I started too. Lord knows he deserved it. I mean the nerve of him after all this time. Ava Justine Gentry, I know it's taken me thirteen years to truly see you, but I love you. Blah, blah." I mock. "The only reason he even knew my middle name is because I'd just told him. The Negro doesn't even know my birthday."

"Well, I'm happy you finally stood up for yourself. I've always thought you could do better."

"Why didn't you say anything?"

"I did, you never heard me, so I stopped because it wasn't my place to try and convince you to leave." She tells me.

"Shouldn't it be though?" I ask sitting up. "As my friend, if you saw me inside a burning house would you warn me or let me stay hoping I'll make it out without being hurt or dying?"

"Of course, I would warn you, but it'll be up to you to get out. Ava, I'm not behind the closed doors of your relationship. I only see what you show me and from the outside looking in, it didn't look like you were ready to leave." She sits up. "If I kept badgering you to leave before you were ready, it could have ruined our friendship."

"I wouldn't have let it." I say with tears.

"I hope not." She touches my hand. "I watch My 600 Pound Life. Sometimes a person shows up expecting to be approved for surgery immediately because the doctor sees they're overweight. Instead, he doesn't because although they're in need of surgery that can potentially save their life, they have to be mentally and physically prepared for it. You want to know why?"

I nod.

"They've carried the weight for however long and it becomes a part of them. Even though their mouth says, yes, I'm ready to remove the weight, their mind and heart may say different when it comes time too. Therefore, they have to shoulder the responsibility of wanting to lose said weight by putting forth an effort."

"Yes, but the doctor gives advice he knows works."

"True, but the doctor gives because they ask. Unsolicited advice is never received well, especially from friends."

"You're right and I'm sorry if I insinuated you haven't been a friend. You've been more to me than anyone has my entire life. Please forgive me."

She crawls over, giving me a hug.

"I'll always be here for you."

*****

Two weeks later, Penelope and I are overseeing the set up for our lunch meeting with Michael Stanton and Levar Wilson, owners of Small Sticks. My research found they love soul food, but with a healthier twist since diabetes run in their families. We decided on a new restaurant not far from the office called Edna's. For appetizers, I chose grilled green tomatoes caprese and warm corn dip with jalapenos. The main course is baked turkey wings, collard greens and sweet potatoes with sweet tea.

"Good afternoon. It's nice to see each of you again." Penelope greets them. "This is my colleague, Ava Gentry."

I wave.

"Good afternoon." One of them says. "Man, it does smell good in here. My stomach started growling the moment we walked in." He laughs. "I'm Michael, this is Levar, and this is one of our attorneys, Charmaine Rutherford."

"It's nice to meet each of you. In keeping with the tradition of the South and y'all's love for soul food, we hope lunch today will be acceptable and pleasing." I tell them. "Please have a seat and help yourself to the appetizers." I advise. "We'll get started soon."

Twenty minutes later, Penelope begins the meeting, starting with the success of Ruthie and Associates. Looking around the room, I can tell by the mannerisms of the gentlemen they only took the meeting to be cordial and have no plans of selling.

We take a break when the food is served to eat. Once lunch is done, we continue.

"May I speak frankly?" I blurt.

"Please." Michael states placing his napkin over the plate.

"I can tell you all aren't interested in selling to Ruthie and Associates and maybe you took the meeting to be cordial, to weigh the options or simply to enjoy the food." I smile. "Whatever the case, Small Sticks is needed in the area of diabetic medicine."

"We agree, but I can't see selling to a company who's going to turn around and sell it to the highest bidder. If it was about money, we could have sold for twenty percent more than what you're offering."

Levar pauses pulling a device the size of a USB from his bag. He inserts it into his phone and begins to describe how it works before passing it to me. "We started Small Sticks for my sister and his daughter who both live with diabetes and find it hard to do the simplest task of checking their blood sugar at school or sporting events. Our device was created to take away the stress and embarrassment of having an illness. It's also an affordable option for people, especially those who can't afford their diabetic supplies."

"Selling to a billion-dollar company who'll auction it to the highest bidder for profit can't do that." Michael adds.

"Then why waste our time?" Penelope tensely inquires. "If you all knew selling to Ruthie and Associates was never an option, why continue to drag us along."

"Ms. Henshaw, we won't apologize for wanting the best for our product even if that means making you do your job."

"And two business meetings hardly qualify as dragging you along. We made our wishes clear from the very beginning, yet you thought you could change our mind because you've yet to actually listen to us. Please understand Ms., you aren't doing us a favor. God gave us the vision and we know He'll also provide the finances." Levar standing. "Thank you for lunch and if it's that big of a deal, we can pay our part."

"Wait. Allow me to apologize for the tone this meeting has taken. Mr. Wilson, we aren't trying to change your mind. However, I meant what I said about the need for your device. What about a partnership?" I offer causing Penelope's head to snap in my direction.

"Partnership?" Michael repeats. "I didn't think it was an option."

"It wasn't, but I believe this can be beneficial for the both of us. Ruthie and Associates can put up the funding to manufacture the devices with a three-year repayment plan, along with a thirty-five percent of revenue and buy-out option in seven years. Of course, this isn't set in stone."

"But it's a starting point." Charmaine states looking between Michael and Levar.

"Will you give us a chance to speak to our management team and set another meeting to discuss?"

"Sure."

"May I keep this?" I ask holding up the device.

"Please. Here's my card. Send me your email and I'll forward you access to the app." Levar states.

"Thank you."

We all stand, shaking hands and I walk them to the door.

"Ava, it was really nice to meet you." Levar says lingering.

"You as well. We'll be in touch."

"What was that?" Penelope questions throwing things on the table. "You had no right to offer that. Ruthie and Associates don't partner, we buy and sell."

"It wasn't an offer, just a suggestion."

"Still wasn't your place." She states angrily grabbing her things.

"Oh but having me tag along as the only black face of Ruthie and Associates to lock in black clients is."

Her face turns red.

"It's cool, however don't ever tell me what my place is. You told me I had bargaining power."

"You do."

"Then I exercised it."

chapter nineteen

"You did what?" Roger yells in the conference room with Jack, Haden, Penelope, and Bobby from legal.

"She offered them a partnership." Penelope says acting like a child snitching on a sibling.

"No, I suggested." I correct rolling my eyes at her. "However, hear me out." I walk to the head of the table. "Small Sticks has created a device to modernize testing for children and adults living with diabetes. This small stick houses everything one will need to test their glucose levels from anywhere as long as they have their phones. Not only that, it's also affordable for people who may not have health insurance."

"How does this benefit us?" Roger asks.

"Michael and Levar aren't looking to sale, and neither is it about the money." I add.

"It's always about the money." Penelope gripes.

"Then why hasn't their stance changed since your first meeting? Roger, they weren't looking to sale, no matter how many meetings we have. However, they need funding. I get Ruthie and Associates is a financially stable company and the revenue from Small Sticks is only a small drop in the bucket, but it's an investment into the future."

"What did you suggest?" Haden asks.

"Funding to manufacture the devices with a three-year repayment plan, along with receiving thirty-five percent of the revenue and a add in buy-out option for them in seven years."

"Bobby?" Jack looks over.

"With a little tweaking of the numbers, it's something to think about." He answers. "You all have been trying to find something else to invest in."

"What happens if these devices don't sell?" Penelope answers.

"Ruthie and Associates would have never poached a company they didn't think was profitable." I assert. "Again, it was only a suggestion."

"Penelope, you've been working this client for over two months. What do you think?" Haden asks her.

"I think we cut our losses and move on. We buy to sell, not fund."

"That doesn't change." I add. "It's not like we'll be running their company, only investing with a return."

"Are you only advocating because it's a black owned company or because you believe it's beneficial?" she asks.

I smile. "Did you only ask me to join because I'm black or because you believe I could be beneficial to the team?"

"It wasn't my choice." She sarcastically replies.

"Neither should this be. Roger, I won't apologize for the suggestion nor continue to plead the case. Read over the research and decide for yourselves. Are we done?"

He nods.

"You gentlemen have a great rest of the afternoon."

Walking into my office, I close the door and do a happy dance for standing my ground. A knock on the door stops me.

"Come in."

"You're new here, so allow me to tell you the unwritten rule. Don't fuck with me because going against me won't end well for you." Penelope barks. "I'm the superior here."

"Wow, and here I thought this was a job and not some high school popularity contest. Well, since we're making things clear. Sis, you don't scare me."

"Yes, I do." She laughs. "See, around here, I'm privileged and you're the help. Unlike me, the help can be replaced like all the ones before you who tried to assert their authority because sis, I always win. From now on, you do what I say."

"Or what?"

"Or you'll be replaced, no questions asked."

I laugh while sitting at my desk. "Girl, you bring your pale white tail in here to scare me and the best you can do is pull out your privilege card. You do know they sell those on Amazon, right? Man, I'm disappointed." I shake my head. "Surely, Bubba'nem taught you to hit'em where it hurts when whipping out that card, and you come in here with this. I bet your great granddaddy is rolling over in his grave."

"Take this as a joke—

"No, I take you as the joke. Now, if you'll excuse me. I have work to do."

She huffs grabbing the handle of the door.

"Oh, Penelope." She turns back. "The Help was a great movie and as I recall, the privileged ended up eating feces. Shall I bring pie tomorrow?"

"This isn't over."

Later on, I'm in my office with the song *Tell Him* by *Lauryn Hill* playing through my Bluetooth speaker.

"Now I may have faith to make mountains fall, but if I lack love then I am nothin' at all. I can give away everything I possess but left without love then I have no happiness. I know I'm imperfect and not without sin, but now that I'm older, all childish things end. And tell him, tell him I need him. Tell him I love him, and it'll be alright. Tell him, tell him I need him, tell him I love him. It'll be alright."

I turn, putting my elbows on the desk covering the tears falling.

"Ava?"

I quickly spin in my chair, turning my back to Jack.

"I didn't know anyone was still here."

"Are you okay? Did something happen?"

"I'm fine." I respond stopping the music and standing, preparing to get my things.

"You're not fine. Talk to me. Please."

"No, don't do that."

"I'm only trying to console an old friend. Nothing more."

"We aren't friends Jack, you're my boss."

"You know what I mean." He states.

"No, I know what you said and if I've learned anything in this life, it's to not expect more from people than what their actions show."

He sighs. "Are you ever going to forgive me?"

"I have." I start to walk past him and he grabs my arm.

"Don't." I look at him in the eyes. "The last thing I need is somebody thinking I got this job because of you. Have a great night."

chapter twenty

"Ava, it's nice to see you again." Dr. Greene says. "How have you been?"

"Better, actually."

"Good. Tell me about it."

"I've moved into a new place, started a new job and I've been studying my Bible more. I've also started to fast at the end of each month. Oh, my current ex proposed to me, and I found out my new boss is an old ex who left me pregnant and at the bus stop when I was eighteen. Oh, oh, the lady on my job threatened me with her white privilege card because I did what I was hired to do."

"That's a lot."

"Who you telling." I laugh.

"How are you coping with all of this?"

"Um, I'm not drinking, acting out or kissing anybody else's husband so, I guess as best I can."

She smirks.

"In all seriousness, Dr. Greene, I'm taking things as they come."

"Taking things as they come means you're in a constant state of waiting. Almost as if you're bracing yourself for the other shoe to drop. When you do this, you take the joy out of the blessings." She tells me.

"Doesn't the Bible say we should wait though?" I question.

"Do you have your phone?"

"I do."

"Go to a site called openbible.info/topics and type in waiting."

"I'm there."

"If you may notice, the majority of those scriptures tells us to wait on God. "The Lord is good to those who wait for Him, to the soul who seeks Him. It is good that one should wait quietly for the salvation of the Lord." Lamentations, three, twenty-five and twenty-six. "Our soul waits for the Lord; he is our help and our shield." Psalm thirty-three and twenty. "Rejoice in hope, be patient in tribulation, be constant in prayer." Romans twelve and twelve. Now, type in trouble."

"Okay."

""Do not be anxious about anything, but in everything by prayer and supplication with thanksgiving let your requests be made known to God." Philippians four and six. My point is, yes, there are times we wait and most of those are whether we want to or not. However, trouble is never something we should wait on or for. Do you have a spare tire in your car?"

"Yes."

"Why?

"In case of a flat."

"But why not wait until a flat happens?" she asks.

"Because I don't know when it—oh, I get it."

"Trouble is like a flat tire. We don't know when it'll happen, and neither can we stop it, yet we don't sit around and wait for it. All we can do is be as prepared as we can."

"How do you prepare for trouble?"

"By being prayed up before it comes, realizing even trouble has an expiration date. Then when it does show up, don't be anxious but be steadfast and strong enough to still seek God because your faith tells you to trust God."

"I hear you and God knows I'm trying to get there, but it's hard. Dr. Greene, it seems all I have to talk about is the struggle of my life."

"It'll seem like this when struggle is all you've experienced. However, you can change the story whenever you choose. After all, it's your story to tell. Ava, what do you want?"

I sigh. "Light."

"Elaborate."

"As a little girl, every morning my grandfather would wake me up by opening the curtains in my room. When I'd open my eyes, he'd be standing there with the warmest smile and his arms open to receive me. Afterwards, he'd make sure all the curtains were opened, filling the house with natural light from outdoors, it didn't matter if it was cloudy, and I loved it. When my mother died, he'd still do it, but less frequently. Then my grandmother passed away and he stopped all together. The house once filled with love, inviting and warm became hateful, dark, and cold. Dr. Greene, I need light."

"Then get up every day intentionally opening the curtains. Not only physically, but mentally as well. Make it up, in your mind, to never live another day in darkness. Even when you're going through a hard time, open the curtains, believing things will get better. Let's pray."

We both stand.

"God, thank you. Thank you for the ability, mental faculties, and strength to open the curtains. Thank you for giving us another chance to see light especially during darkness. God, thank you for hope which tells us there's life. Now God, continue to make your presence known in the life of Ava. Father, you know all she's endured, yet you've kept her and because you did, we know her story isn't over. Guide, heal, fill, and renovate her life so that when she looks at her reflection, she will see you. Give her the resilience to keep pushing even when the battle is hard, and it doesn't seem worth it. And Father, handle her enemies. Stutter the speech of those speaking death to her purpose, cripple the hands of those seeking to do her harm, confuse those who will try to trip her up and close the door to her past. God, we don't always know what you're doing, yet we trust you and we'll walk by faith until you reveal your plans to us. In the name of Jesus, we pray. Amen."

"Amen. Thank you, Dr. Greene. I'll see you at my next appointment."

chapter twenty-one

Getting ready to leave the house, the doorbell rings. I open it to a young man.

"Are you Ava?"

"I am."

"These are for you." He hands me a vase of red roses before beginning to sing. "It's like I missed a shot, it's like I dropped the ball. It's like I'm on stage, and I forgot the words. It's like building a new house with no roof and no doors. It's like trying to propose, and I ain't got the ring. But girl I've apologized a million times before so here it comes again. For all the wrong I've done, here's one million one."

"Sir. SIR." I yell to stop him. "Thank you, but I have to get to work."

I close the door, snatching the card from the flowers.

Ava, I've made a lot of mistakes but the biggest one was letting you go. Please forgive me. Andre.

I sit the flowers on the kitchen counter to deal with after work because I cannot be late. Although it has taken over two months, today we're finalizing the deal with

Small Sticks, and I couldn't be more excited. Yet, it didn't come without mess and a whole lot of it. By mess I mean the complaints I've had to file with HR about Penelope who has been working nonstop to make things hostile. Yet, I am not allowing her to take my joy. Even when she overtalks me in meetings with clients and questions everything I do, I smile.

Walking into my office, I see Haden, Grace from HR, Bobby from legal and a security guard.

"Good morning. I hope you all are here to finally address my complaints."

"Good morning, Ava. Please have a seat." Grace says.

"I take that as a no."

"When you were hired, did you read all of the documents including company guidelines and policies?"

"I did."

"Then you are aware of the clause that states, you are to make HR aware of any intimate relationships with members of seniority, especially those you report too?"

"I am."

"Yet, we were notified of the inappropriate relationship with you and a member of management."

I catch a glimpse of Penelope outside the door.

"Let me guess. This notification was by the company bully who's standing outside."

"We're not at liberty to disclose the identity of those who file reports. Are you engaged in an intimate relationship with a member of management?"

"No."

"Is it true you knew Mr. Jackson Kingston before you started working here?"

"I met Jack when I was seventeen years old. However, we haven't seen, spoken or had any form of contact in almost twenty years."

"Did you know our family owned this company beforehand?" Haden asks.

"No, and even if I did, how would that have benefited me?"

"Maybe you're here to get revenge on him for breaking your heart." He states.

"How, by stealing a stapler and copy paper? This is ridiculous."

"Or by getting us to partner with a company who could hurt our image, reputation and bottom line."

I laugh, standing up. "You can't be serious? You were already in talks with this company before you hired me, or do you think I magically made that happen as well. God! Did either of you stop to truly think this through or are y'all high from drinking Penelope's Kool-Aid?"

"Ava, we're only doing our job." Bobby says.

"That's a joke seeing the numerous complaints I've filed haven't been addressed, yet here y'all are when she goes running with this asinine claim of something going on with me and Jack."

"We're looking into yours as well. Nevertheless, there are witness statements to Mr. Kingston being in your office after hours on more than one occasion."

"And? I'm sure my office isn't the only one he's been in nor is it illegal. Besides, he's been in my office twice and both times the door was open. Have y'all even asked Jack because he'll tell you the same thing?"

"Mr. Kingston is out of the country at the moment. In the meantime, we'll have to investigate the claim. While we do, you'll be suspended with pay and we'll be in touch with our findings."

"Suspended?" I laugh. "Is this high school or a business? What about the meeting?"

"It's being postponed for now." Haden states getting up.

I shake my head while grabbing my things. "I refuse to let y'all or Satan steal my joy. However, white privilege doesn't stop the seeds you sow from being reaped."

"What does that mean?" Haden angrily inquires.

"Karma's a bitch and she always comes for what she's owed."

Three days later, I receive a box with my personal items and a certified letter with termination papers. Throwing them down on the coffee table. I fall back on the couch.

"God, give me strength to overcome every obstacle in my path, distraction that tries to detour me, and darkness trying to devour me. Father, deal with my enemies, returning everything they try to take and repairing all they seek to destroy. I am yours and I trust you, even through this. Amen."

Two weeks later while in the kitchen preparing dinner, the doorbell rings. Opening the camera app, I see Jack standing on the porch.

"Jack, how did you know where I lived?" I ask after opening the door.

"Your personnel file which I know was a mistake to do, but may I come in?"

I step back. "You're a few weeks too late, aren't you?"

"It smells good in here."

"Shoot, my salmon." I rush into the kitchen pulling the cast iron skillet off the eye.

After washing my hands and adding butter, garlic, and brussels sprouts to it, I place it in the oven before turning back to him.

"You were saying."

"Yes, I know my timing isn't ideal, but I was on a mission trip with my church and had limited access to what was going on here. However, the moment I found out you were fired over lies Penelope spread, I was furious. On top of that, the deal with Small Sticks didn't happen and now, they aren't willing to even talk to us. Ava, I'm sorry. Had I been here, I could have stopped this."

"You still can by letting them know she lied."

He looks away and I laugh.

"Right, as if I should have expected you to stand up for me. Well, thanks for the apology. I don't want to hold you up. You may need to get to the meeting of the white privilege society."

"I'm not like them. Here." He hands me an envelope. "I got your job back."

"You got my job back." I repeat. "A job which allows one woman to make life miserable for those she feels is beneath her. A job which takes the word of that same woman without a second thought. Thanks, but no. We both know nothing will be different and I'll only be buying time until she forces me to quit. However, I'm glad you stopped by. I have something for you too." I go into my home office coming back with a packet.

"What's this?"

"The discrimination lawsuit my attorney filed against Ruthie and Associates this morning. See, I was going to walk away because I was sick of dealing with Penelope and spineless executives who won't do anything about her. What does she have on y'all anyway? Don't answer, I don't care. Nonetheless, I changed my mind. I'm tired of people walking over me and doing whatever they want without regards for how I feel. I'm fed up with men who take, never give nor pay back. From now on, I'm putting Ava first, no longer sparing people's feelings, including yours."

"I'm sorry."

"For what?"

"For everything." He says looking down at the floor.

I chuckle. "Dude, if you can't be specific, then your apology isn't sincere. So, keep your empty apology playa and get out of my house because my dinner is waiting." I go over and open the door. "Have a great night Mr. Kingston."

My alarm goes off at 3 AM for the last-minute cruise I decided to take to get away for a few days. My flight is leaving at 5:45 AM and I needed to make sure I have everything. Sitting my bag by the kitchen door, the sound of the doorbell startles me. Quickly opening the app, I see a Memphis Police officer. Unarming the alarm, I rush to the door.

"Ava, I'm sorry to have woken you."

"Clay, what's going on? What happened?"

"It's Andre. I need you to come with me."

chapter twenty-two

Sliding the door back to Andre's room, I walk inside to see him scrolling on his phone. I pop him with the discharge papers from the nurse. "Nigguh, you really had Clay show up on my doorstep for a freaking sprained ankle? I should have known if Clay was there, it was nothing serious."

"It is serious. I was shot too."

"It's a graze." I yell before taking a deep breath.

"I'm sorry, but it was the only way I could make sure you showed up."

"Did you ever stop for one second to think what seeing him would do to me?" I swipe the tears anger was causing to fall. "You're a selfish, narcissistic, good for nothing piece of crap who takes nobody else's feelings into consideration. He's on my doorstep at four in the freaking morning, in full uniform with lights flashing making me think you'd been killed?"

"I said I was sorry and you're right, I didn't think this through. However, in my defense, I was traumatized and you're the first person I wanted."

"No, I'm the only person you have besides your mammy who must be with her church group because I'm sure if she was here, I wouldn't be. Especially since she seems to believe I've leeched off you all this time."

"That's not true."

I laugh. "Whatever. Goodbye Andre. You've made me miss my flight." I turn back to him. "Did you do this because you knew I was going out of town?"

"How would I know what you have planned? Ava, I sent Clay because I need you. The doctor says I need to be off my ankle for two weeks and I don't have anyone else."

"Not my problem."

"Please Ava. Look, I know you've moved on with your little clear boyfriend and I'm not trying to interfere with that, but baby, I need you."

"You are interfering with it. Hold on, my clear boyfriend. Are you watching me? I ask realizing he's talking about Jack."

He shrugs.

"The answer is no."

"No?" he questions.

"Yes."

He smiles.

"Yes, the answer is no. The same two letters that spells on, as in I'm on my way out. Find another sucker because my days of puckering up for the likes of you are over." I tell him as Clay walks in. "And Negro, you had the audacity to show up at my house making me think something bad had happened to this trick. I ought to report both of you to Internal Affairs. Take me home."

Getting home, I throw a finger sign at Clay and slam the door. I call Southwest Airlines to check for additional flights that can get me to Miami in time to be on the boat. I don't know what I was thinking flying in on the same day.

"Ugh." I yell ending the call with no luck. After a shower, I get into bed, turning on Pandora from the Bluetooth speaker. A song begins to play.

"I just gotta believe there is goodness around the corner, and something better is in store for me. Someday I will see there's a reason for all these tears and there's an answer to these prayers. I just gotta believe. This can't be the end. I know that there is so much more, and I will find an open door, if I only believe that this is just one page in my story and if I keep breathing and if I keep believing."

"Lord, I believe, but it's hard. So hard." I sob. "I just have to keep breathing and believing." I inhale and exhale. "Keep breathing Ava."

*****

A few weeks later, I open the front door to Jack. Again.

"Ava, thank you for seeing me. May I come in?"

I step back.

"Let me guess, you're here to ask me to drop the lawsuit?"

"No. In fact, I'm here to discuss a settlement. Ava, we were wrong in the way we handled your complaints against Penelope and on behalf of Ruthie and Associates, we're sorry. You had no right to be fired."

"Your doggone right about all of it, yet your sorry doesn't fix it." I state. "You all set quiet in meetings while she tried to embarrass me by overtalking or undermining everything I said or did. Y'all saw how she treated me and did nothing. Even when I went to HR, it was swept under the rug because of "white privilege."" I put in air quotes. "Not only did you allow them to fire me over some bogus relationship with you, I've also been blackballed from being hired by any reputable company. I've had six interviews, and nobody will hire me. Do you think it's a coincidence?"

"What can I do?" he asks walking closer to me.

"Unless that settlement check you hold contains a whole lot of zeroes, you can get the hell out of my house."

He hands me the envelope. I tear it open and laugh.

"Fifty thousand? Are you serious? Dude, I ought to punch you in the face." I go over and open the door. "For months I cried myself to sleep over how broken you left me and the emptiness of what I thought you and I could have been. When I miscarried our baby in the shower of my dorm, and as blood poured from my body, my first thought was how you'd feel. You." I scream.

"It didn't matter the pain I was in or the loss I was experiencing. I was thinking of you. The deserter who left me without as much as a letter. Now though, I thank God you didn't show up that night. Here, I kept thinking I was missing something when it was God blocking me from a boy with no backbone or confidence. You not showing up, twenty years ago, almost destroyed me. However, this woman," I point to myself, "she knows her worth and is demanding every doggone dollar of it. And boo, it's far more than those four zeroes. You may want to tell daddy before y'all show up for court. Goodbye Jack."

He stops in front of me with tears in his eyes. "I didn't know you were pregnant, or I would have been there for you."

"Well, I didn't know you, so I guess we're even."

"Ava, I wish things could have been different between us. You may not believe this, but I did love you. Truthfully, a part of me still does. You're the only woman who wasn't distracted by the fancy clothes and money. You pushed me to dream beyond what my parents wanted for me. Being with you, I was allowed to be Jack without the privilege or prestige. I miss him." He sighs then touch my face. "I'm sorry Ava."

"Get your hand off my woman."

chapter twenty-three

I turn at the sound of Andre's voice and roll my eyes.

"Goodbye Jack."

He glares at Andre then leaves.

"I thought you weren't seeing anybody."

"What have I told you about a. showing up at my house and b. questioning anything going on?" I ask stepping onto the porch, and he moves back. "Wow. You've seemed to have miraculously healed seeing it's only been two weeks." I point to the supposedly sprained ankle.

"Physical therapy worked wonders. Praise Jesus." He mocks.

"Dre, what do you want?"

"Look Ava, I didn't come to argue. Can we talk?" he asks.

I sit in one of the chairs on the porch. "No, I'm not coming back to you. We're over. Nice conversation. Take care." I stand.

"I don't want you back."

My head snaps around. "Finally, and it only took five months. This was a great discussion. Take care."

"Wait, that came out wrong. I don't want you back, right now because I want to court you."

I laugh. "Court me? Dude, this isn't 1957 and you're years too late. No."

"You haven't even given me a chance to explain."

"Why is it men expect women to listen to their explanation for something that never should have happened in the first place? But you know what. You're right." I sit back, crossing my legs. "Go ahead."

"When we met, we were both in a bad place. I'd just gotten divorced from Patricia who made my life a living hell. That broad with her high yellow, tom boy looking—"

"Andre, focus."

"Right. Anyway, we were both in a bad headspace and I thought moving on was the best thing, but I was wrong because I took everything out on you. My frustration from the previous relationship kept me from getting to truly know you. I treated you like you were the one who'd hurt me by disrespecting and taking advantage of your kindness. In some way, I think you did the same. Which is why I want us to start over."

"What alcohol bottle did you get that from?"

He sighs. "I started seeing a therapist."

"Willingly?"

"Well, my captain suggested it, but I'm the one who goes which counts for something."

I let out a laugh. "Who's counting though?"

"Why is it so hard for you to believe I'm changing? People can change, you know. Babe, all I want is another chance. I realize when I asked you to marry me it wasn't the right time, yet I'm willing to wait however long it takes. Last night I was going through some things in my closet and found this picture." He pulls it from his pocket. "We used to do stuff like this all the time."

"This was the night we went to the Fair."

"Do you remember how much fun we had?" his face lights us.

"Yeah, until I embarrassed you by not being able to fit inside the Ferris Wheel seat." I throw it back to him. "However, you're right. People can change. I just don't believe you're one of them."

"Man, you just won't let up. You and that fat ass mouth of yours is always ruining things then you wonder why I lash out. You don't know when to shut up."

"And there he is." I stand. "Andre, there's a difference between memorizing what someone tells you and actually putting it to work. Yet I know you and I've seen you talk your way out of department ordered therapy a few times and this is no different. You're only saying the right things in the hope it benefits you. You don't love me."

"I'm trying, but dang you make it hard. Standing here criticizing me as if you're perfect since you got this little funky townhouse. Without it, you would have crawled back weeks ago begging me to let you stay and it's only a matter of time before unemployment runs out and you can't afford it. Truth be told, if I rub you in the right places, I can have you on your back or riding big daddy into the sunset and you know it." He grabs his crotch. "Your address may have changed, but you're still that broken little girl who sleeps with a night light beside the bed."

"Are you done throwing a tantrum or shall I wait?"

"Whatever Ava."

"No, it's whatever Andre. You're in your feelings because I won't bow down, kiss the ring and be the doormat you're used to. Well, doggone it I'm tired of paying for trusting you with my life. Yes, we were having sex, but it was for my satisfaction because you're all I've had my entire adult life. Yes, I was broken when I met you, but when will you recognize I'm not that girl anymore. I've spent my whole life being abused by men. Hell, it started with my mother before I was born which tainted the blood line running through my veins, but it stops with me. I was almost destroyed, but you and the enemy let me wake up and learn my worth. Now, I'm almost healed and I won't let you or a devil in hell or earth take it without a fight."

"Oh, I see what this is. You think white boy Charlie is going to sweep you off your feet and you'll live happily ever after, huh. Is he the one paying for this place?"

"Think whatever you want."

"It won't be long before he stops paying you to sleep with him because we both know he can't take you home to daddy."

"Are you done?"

"Forget you, Ava."

"I pray you do."

When he gets to the steps, I call his name and he turns back. "As for the big daddy reference, it easy to believe that when I have nothing to compare it to."

He throws the middle finger before almost falling down the steps.

chapter twenty-four

Weeks have passed and I still don't have a job. Rolling over, I turn off the alarm before it has a chance to go off. Today is the arbitration meeting with Ruthie and Associates and my nerves are all over the place. After a shower and getting dressed, I go into my prayer corner. Opening my journal to the scriptures I jotted down last night while studying Isaiah fifty-four which talks about the future glory for Jerusalem.

This book opens describing Jerusalem's plight as that of a childless woman. Yet even while in verse one, Isaiah tells them to sing and shout because the Lord says the desolate woman now has more children than a woman who lives with her husband. He instructs them to build an addition on your house, sparing no expense because it'll soon be bursting at the seams.

""Fear not; you will no longer live in shame. Don't be afraid; there is no more disgrace for you. You will no longer remember the shame of your youth and the sorrows of widowhood. For your Creator will be your husband, the LORD of Heaven's Armies is his name! He is your Redeemer, the Holy One of Israel, the God of all the earth. For the LORD has called you back from your

grief—as though you were a young wife abandoned by her husband," says your God." I read aloud. "But in that coming day no weapon turned against you will succeed. You will silence every voice raised up to accuse you. These benefits are enjoyed by the servants of the LORD; their vindication will come from me. I, the LORD, have spoken!"

I close my eyes, clasping my hands before me.

"Dear God, here am I before you, empty and in need of being refilled. Lord, I won't list all I've been through because you've been with me even if I didn't acknowledge your presence. You kept breathing life into me when I wanted to die. You shielded me when I faced danger from my own stupid decisions. You provided for me on days I wouldn't even tell you thank you. You did more for me than I deserved, and it wasn't because of me. Father, thank you. Thank you for forgiving me and giving me the chance to repent again. Thank you for receiving me back into your care.

Now God, you know what I'm up against today, yet I put my faith in you. Father, I feel like David when he was listening to the taunting of Goliath. While I may not have five stones in my bag, give me the strength to defeat the giants seeking to do me harm. I have to believe things will work in my favor. Lord, I've spent too much time without you leading and now, I give you permission to have your way for today and every day I submit myself to you. In the name of Jesus, I declare it done. Amen."

An hour later, I park outside my attorney's office listening to *Nothing's Impossible* by *William McDowell.*

Anything is possible, you're the God of miracles. Everything we speak by faith we're gonna see. There is nothing you can't do. Every word you say is true. Lord, you've never failed, your people will prevail. We're not afraid of giants because they always fall. Lord, we know you hear us every time we call.

"God with you, anything is possible."

I walk into Baker and Dubose and the receptionist leads me to Jamia's office.

I tap on her door.

"Good morning." She smiles. "I hope you've had your coffee because I'm ready to wipe the smug grin off their faces." She points to the conference room before taking her seat. "We have ten minutes. Let me show you what we're asking for."

"This is ridiculous." Mr. Castro barks after looking at the terms of our settlement agreement once the meeting has begun. "You were an employee for three months and you expect a payout of double your yearly salary with health benefits."

"It wasn't her choice and that's just for the wrongful termination." Jamia counters. "My client was fired after being threatened by one, Penelope Henshaw. The same person she filed multiple complaints against for hostile work conditions which leads us to believe she was retaliated against. Mr. Castro, your company had a due diligence to investigate my client's claim. Instead, you all conjured up a nonexistent relationship as a means to terminate her without warning or substantial proof. Therefore we are suing for wrongful termination and discrimination. You may want to turn the page."

"Your client was fired for an inappropriate and undisclosed relationship with her boss for which we have proof sweetie."

"I'm not your sweetie. My name is J-A-M-I-A Dubose. The name on the door and building. I suggest you use it. Now, where's your proof of this alleged relationship."

He pulls out pieces of paper.

"Mr. Reith," he refers to the arbitrator, "these witness statements have been entered into evidence, indicating the scope of the relationship between Ms. Gentry and Mr. Kingston."

"Mr. Castro, if those statements prove the guilt of my client, then we can all assume Mr. Kingston is also guilty, right? Does this mean he was also fired for being in an inappropriate and undisclosed relationship with his employee?"

"Heavens no. He owns the company."

"So, you're showing favoritism?"

"That's not what I said." He angrily replies.

"It's implied Mr. Castro when one party is held liable and not the other. Unless my client was fired for other reasons like discrimination and retaliation for standing up for herself. Isn't it true, Mr. Castro, that out of the one hundred plus employees of Ruthie and Associates, minorities account for about twenty percent with the majority being cleaning and maintenance?"

"We are not here to discuss their hiring practices."

"Yet, it plays into my client's lawsuit of your company's discriminatory practices."

"Answer the question." Mr. Reith orders.

"Uh," Castro fumbles with papers. "I don't have the definitive numbers."

"I do." Jamia slides papers across the table. "In the last five years, your company has terminated three minority men and women whenever they've complained to management or filed complaints with human resources. However, that's not what piqued my interest. It's the fact, all of them worked alongside Penelope Henshaw and their complaints were against her."

"Is this true Mr. Castro?" the arbitrator asks.

"Yes, but they are not part of this lawsuit and have no bearing on these proceedings. Ms. Gentry was terminated because of her inappropriate relationship. One we can prove by the word of Jackson Kingston himself."

He pushes a sheet of paper across the table with a smirk on his face. I snatch it.

I, Jackson Samuel Kingston, hereby declare the statement I am about to give is the truth. I met Ava Gentry when we were both seventeen years old and had not seen nor heard from her since that time. Upon learning she was hired at Ruthie and Associates, she and I reconnected in an intimate manner, exploring the possibility of a relationship. It was never our intentions to keep this hidden from management, but we never got the chance to report it and for that I am deeply sorry.

chapter twenty-five

"This is a bold face lie." I yell. "Jamia, this is a lie. The last time I had any kind of personal interaction with Jack I was eighteen. There was no reconnection between us."

"We also have pictures of Mr. Kingston being at your home. Are these also fabricated?"

I pick up the pictures of the first night Jack showed up at my house and the last time when he touched my face.

Jamia looks at me.

"Jack showed up to my house to apologize for being fired. He was there maybe five minutes. And this picture, he came to offer me a check for fifty thousand to drop the lawsuit. He touched my face when he was leaving. You can ask my ex, Andre because he was there."

I slide the pictures back to him.

"How did he know where you lived?" Mr. Reith inquires.

"He got my address from the personnel file."

"Isn't that against policy, Mr. Castro?"

"If she can prove it." Castro smirks.

"There was no relationship between Mr. Kingston and me. That is the truth." I tell the room.

"And you think he'd lie on a sworn document for nothing?"

"He'd do anything his daddy tells him, even if it's lying to win this case." I state. "Nonetheless, we both know the truth and I'm not going to be hushed by you or the Kingston family. I was fired for being the wrong color in a white dominated corporation who throws their privilege around like candy in a Mardi Gras Parade. Had I been the good house nigger and kept my mouth closed, doing what I was told, being seen and not heard, we wouldn't be here."

"That's enough Ms. Gentry."

Jamia touches my hand.

"Mr. Reith, I'm inclined to agree with my client as we have video evidence of the bullying and threats made weeks before she was terminated. May I?"

"Please." Mr. Reith replies.

Jamia turns her computer around, pressing the spacebar to start the video.

"You're new here, so allow me to tell you the unwritten rule. Don't fuck with me because going against me won't end well for you." Penelope barks. "I'm the superior here."

"Wow, and here I thought this was a job and not some high school popularity contest. Well, since we're making things clear. Sis, you don't scare me."

"Yes, I do." She laughs. "See, around here, I'm privileged and you're the help. The help can be replaced like all the ones before you who tried to assert their authority because sis, I always win. From now on, you do what I say."

"Or what?"

"Or you'll be replaced, no questions asked."

"That proves nothing." Castro barks.

"It isn't the only one. Mr. Reith, Ruthie and Associates has a track record of willingly allowing a bully to wear a badge, casting a domineering presence over those she feels is beneath her. We too have witness statements from former employees who will say the same. Furthermore, these videos will show there was no intimate relationship between my client and her boss."

She presses the spacebar again and the video of the first time Jack was in my office plays.

"I've seen and heard enough." Mr. Reith states. "I will look over all of the submitted evidence, along with considering everything I've heard today before rendering my decision. If you have additional documentation, please present them today and you will have my rendering within forty-five days."

Getting home, I drop my purse on the kitchen counter, kick off my shoes, open a bottle of wine and go into the living room.

"I feel like a fool." I gulp wine. "Why did I ever think things could work out for me? You gotta believe Ava. Things won't always be like this." I mock drinking more wine. "Bull crap. I call stinking, horse size bull crap." I walk around the living room talking to myself and drinking before angrily kicking the coffee table before yelping in pain, forgetting it's made of stone. I drop the bottle causing wine to spill on the floor.

Quickly picking it up, I rush into the kitchen placing it in the sink. "What more God?" I scream. "How much longer do I have to suffer in this dark place? Haven't I gone through enough? Jesus." I slide onto the floor.

*****

June

I pull up to Ava's house with sushi and rice takeout. I get out and ring the doorbell. No answer. I pull out my phone to call her. "Voicemail." I text, waiting a few minutes with no reply. Something doesn't feel right, so I decide to let myself in.

"Ava? Ava are you home?" I call out, pushing the door open to see wine spilled in the living room. "Ava?" I frantically call out moving to the kitchen to see her leaned against the counter. My stomach drops. "Ava? Babe, what's wrong?" I go over searching to see if she's hurt. "Ava, talk to me. Are you hurt?" I touch her face, turning her to look at me.

"Can you ask God to forgive me because I don't think He can hear me, and I need this cloud to leave? Will you ask Him, please? I just need some light. I'm so tired." She sobs.

"Oh Ava." I sit beside her, pulling her into me. "God forgives you and He hears, even when it feels as though He doesn't."

We sit there another thirty minutes as I listen to her cry. When she gets quiet, I look down to see she's fallen asleep. I don't move. Sometime later, she jumps.

"Ava, you're okay."

She looks around before groaning from the stiffness in her neck.

"June, what are you doing here?"

"Um, we had dinner plans."

"Oh, I forgot but why are we in the floor?" she questions.

"This is where I found you and you were in no condition to be moved, so I joined you."

"How long have we been sitting here?"

I shrug. "About an hour."

"Oh my God, why didn't you wake me? I know your entire body is numb."

"It is." I laugh. "But you needed this and as your friend, I'm willing to sit in your kitchen floor for however long it takes to get you through. Now, help me up."

She throws her arms around me once we're standing. "Thank you and I'm sorry you can't feel your butt."

"Do you feel better?"

"Yes."

"Then stop apologizing because my butt will be fine. Ava, it's okay to be vulnerable around me. Girl, I've been where you are when it feels like trouble has your address memorized and your pain points on speed dial and quoting scriptures didn't help. Sometimes sis, you don't need to be preached to, you need your soul purged with a good cry even if it means sitting for hours in an uncomfortable place."

"Will this ever get easier?"

"What?"

"The things we have to endure?"

"God no. Trouble is never easy, yet it can get easier to handle with the right mechanisms. Here's what I've come to understand. God didn't create us to run from trouble, He created armor for us to withstand it. Do you know what a turtle does when faced with danger? It uses the flexibility of its neck to retract back into the shell because the turtle knows it can't outrun what's trying to hurt it, but inside the shell it's protected. It's the same for us and this is why Bible says in Psalm 119, verse 114, *"You are my hiding place and my shield; I hope in Your word."*

"I've been studying, praying, fasting and trusting God yet it seems like things are getting worse."

"What if they are? Will you still study, pray and trust God?"

"I'm trying, but I don't know if I can survive anything else."

"You will." I tell her.

"How can you be so sure?"

"Because you've survived what almost destroyed you before. Girl, you've been through the death of your mom and grandmother, abuse, neglect, rejection, the loss of jobs, homelessness, and Andre. Surely, you can handle whatever this is. If that isn't enough, you have me and

I'm an oil slanging, tongue speaking, holy ghost filled sister who don't mind laying on my face for you. Child, if I can't pray you through when you can't, what good am I?" I start flinging my arm, speaking in tongue. "See. The devil doesn't want none of this."

She's laughing with water in her eyes.

"I love you." She says wiping her face.

"I love you too. Oh, you're replacing the sushi I left in the car. So, get your wallet and come tell me what happened in the court thingy."

chapter twenty-six

Sunday morning, I walk into Repairers of the Breach Ministries a few minutes before service begins. Heading into the sanctuary, I go down front where I normally sit with Katrina.

"Good morning sis." She pulls me into a hug. "You're looking good this morning."

"Thanks. I feel good." I admit as the music begins. "I believe things are finally turning in my favor."

"And I'm here for it."

"Good morning, Repairers of the Breach. As we prepare to enter into our devotional period, I pray your week has been blessed. I pray God has exceeded every one of your needs. I pray you've called on God and He's answered. I pray for those whose week has been filled with turmoil, chaos, and confusion, letting you know you've come to the right place. Here, in this place is where you can lay down your burdens and God will take them. In this place is where believers gather, touch, and agree through prayer, worship, and God's word because we believe miracles will happen. My brother, my sister, I don't know what you need but thank you showing up. I pray the yoke around your neck will be destroyed and your joy refill. Let's read the word. Psalm eighty-four in its entirety."

After devotion, and prayer, the choir begins to sing a song.

"Let me tell you about a man who knows all of my flaws but still loves me. Let me introduce you to this man who will never bring your past up again. Do you have a minute to listen about the one who can replace all that's missing? There is just something about. I know that I cannot live without Him. He's my healer, my savior, my way maker, my joy, my provider, strong tower, and He gave his life for me. His name is Jesus."

By the time it ends, I'm a weeping mess, leaned over with my head and hands on the back of the pew in front of me. Suddenly, I jump up from my seat. It's like my body can't be controlled. A few minutes later, I'm down on my knees.

"Sweet Jesus, help me please." I beg with my arms outstretched. "I'm tired God."

I feel someone's hands engulf my head as they begin to pray.

"Father, she's home now and that dance was for her freedom, her mind, and her joy. Grant it, God today. She's been through a lot, but we know you still love her. She's done some things that have taken her out of your will, forgive her. She's hidden her heart from you, but now God show her you in this moment. You allowed the Holy Spirit to fill her, don't let Him leave her. Let this cry open the windows of Heaven so she knows she's no longer alone. Let her rest in the peace of you knowing whenever she calls, you'll answer and heal. In the name of Jesus, we decree it so."

Whomever the man is, he moves away. I stay there another few minutes before getting up. Turning, Katrina is there with open arms.

When service is over, Katrina introduces me to her pastor, Dr. Jefferson Hunter.

"Ava, God's word in Psalm eighty-four says, *"For the LORD God is our sun and our shield. He gives us grace and glory. The LORD will withhold no good thing from those who do what is right. O LORD of Heaven's Armies, what joy for those who trust in you."* Your trust has been broken since you were a child, but God says it's time you healed. I don't know what has been, however I know what can be and it starts with trusting God. Ava, the darkness isn't over yet, but don't lose faith while waiting for the light."

I stand there with tears in my eyes. "Thank you, Dr. Hunter."

"Please call me Jefferson. I look forward to seeing you again."

Walking out, Katrina and I decide to have lunch together. Thirty minutes later, we're sitting on the patio of Happy Mexican laughing over margaritas with chips, guacamole, and salsa.

"Let's take a selfie." She says coming over. "Smile. Ooh, that's cute. What's your IG name so I can tag you?"

"It's ava underscore gentry eighty-three."

"You need to post more."

"I know, but I've never been big on social media. Guess, I didn't have a lot to smile about."

"Well, I'm about to airdrop this picture so you can post it. You're beautiful and the glow you're rocking needs to be shared."

We spend a few minutes posting it and a couple more pictures.

"There. Your IG isn't so dry anymore." She laughs.

"Thank you." I tell her.

"For what?"

"Inviting me to church, this, everything. Katrina, I've never felt like I did today. Even now, I'm emotional and on the verge of tears yet it's not for anything sad. Is that crazy?" I ask her.

"Nope. What you experienced and feeling is the Holy Spirit and after an encounter with Him your life will never be the same."

"I believe it because I feel good. Like, um it's like—

"A weight has been lifted." We both say together.

"Yeah." I laugh. "Is this what being in God feels like?"

"Yes, but don't get it twisted because with God comes suffering, we must endure. It doesn't take away the feeling you have now, however when we go through things that hurt, it can hide this." She says waving her hand around. "And you must be willing to survive the struggle, every time, in order to get back to this happy place because it never leaves."

I smile looking out across the parking lot. "Life has been hard, and I've spent most of it angry." I admit glancing back at her. "I was angry at life, and I realize the anger was able to grow because I didn't know God. My family was never big on religion and being shuffled between foster families, there was never anyone who taught me God. By the time I made it to college, I'd turned away from any chance to know Him for myself. Walking into Roundtree Estates that day and meeting you changed how I saw Him. You didn't care about working, you prayed for me in the middle of the kitchen like it was an altar. I'll never be able to repay you."

She reaches across the table and touches my hand. "There's nothing to repay. We all deserve wholeness, happiness, and the chance to experience God. I only did for you what I'd hope someone would do for me if I needed it."

"I'm sorry. Didn't mean to ruin lunch."

"Girl, this is called testifying and I'm here for it. Go on."

"It's just, I, this feeling. Whew." I dab my face with the napkin.

"That's the feeling of making it through what tried to kill you. Doesn't it feel great?"

"Yes," I laugh while wiping tears. "If only I knew how to keep it."

"Baby, that's the hard part yet it can be done with a whole lot of prayer, fasting, faith and works."

"Will you help me?" I ask her.

"I'd be honored. First question, have you been baptized?"

"No."

"Then we'll start there."

chapter twenty-seven

For the next couple of weeks, Katrina and I spend time together studying God's word on baptism, faith, love, tithing, fasting and prayer. When I tell you the enemy has been upping his attacks, believe me. Yet, I've stood my ground with the help of therapy with Dr. Greene who I'm now seeing twice a week and gym time. Last Sunday I joined Repairers of the Breach with plans to be baptized next week and it feels like the best decision I've made in a while.

Andre has been quiet, and I don't know whether to be happy or alert. Either way, I'm no longer allowing him to invade my happiness or peace.

"Nobody greater, nobody greater Lord, nobody greater than you. I searched all over, couldn't find nobody." I sing walking into the house from worship, dropping my purse on the kitchen counter. "Nobody great—oh my God." I shriek at the sight of Andre sitting on my living room couch.

"Andre. What the fu—what are you doing in my house?"

"I've given you space to figure things out without bothering you with calls and text. Even after I allowed you to turn down my proposal, I still waited for you to come to your senses. Yet, it looks like you're trying to build a life without me, and we both know that can't happen." He stands cupping his hands in front of him. "See, you owe me because I sa—

"You didn't save me." I interject. "And I'm sick of hearing it. I was foolish and naïve enough to believe we were in a relationship we'd both contribute to, yet I was the only one giving while you took. Even after you drained me of my dignity and finances and ruined my credit, I still stayed far longer than I should have because longevity replaced loyalty and comfortability took the place of respect. Andre, you destroyed all of my stuff and almost destroyed me in the process. The mere fact you thought I'd ever agree to marry you further proves, it's all about you and not me. It's been thirteen years and we've accomplished nothing fruitful in this relationship and I will not apologize for wanting better."

"So, you think I'm going to let some white dude ride in and take all I've created these past thirteen years? Ava, you'd be nothing without me."

"You're a narcissistic human being who thinks I'm something you built in the woodshed out back. Negro, you couldn't create the color green if I gave you instructions and the colors to mix. You got the audacity to stand in my face spewing this nonsense when you've never encouraged me to do anything good besides what benefited you. All those nights I had to spend sitting in McDonalds, parks, or coffee shops to study because you wouldn't let me do it at "your house" wasn't creating me. You didn't even show up when I graduated college or offered a congratulations when I was promoted. Oh, but you were all smiles when I was signing for loans."

"And I've apologized for that." He yells.

"The only problem. The apology leaves your mouth, but it never reaches your heart. Andre," I sigh, "I'm tired of doing this."

"Then stop fighting me and come home."

"No." I assert. "I'm tired of having this conversation and it's becoming mentally draining. Just let me be. Please." I beg. "Go on with your life and leave me alone. I'm sure one of your sidepieces will be eager to move in."

He jumps up so fast, it startles me. "Does this boy make you happy? Because I ain't never seen you smiling and singing."

"Back up." I tell him and he angrily grabs my hair.

"You've never straightened your hair for me."

"Andre, let me go. Let me go." I shove him. "You don't have the right to question my happiness when all you've ever given is sadness. Besides, you wouldn't have noticed my hair if it was on fire. Please, get out of my house. I'm not the same fat girl with no self-esteem who can be bought with a fancy dinner and empty promises. Neither am I pathetic enough to have to jump from penis to penis. I deserve better and you aren't him."

He laughs. "It doesn't matter how many church services and Bible studies you attend or even getting baptized at the new church nor the weight you lose because you'll always be the fat, broken little girl who cries out for the granddaddy who left scars on her thighs. You ought to be glad I'm willing to give you another chance because nobody else will love you. Your mommy killed herself, old grand mammy drank herself into an early grave and BB, well he couldn't stand to look at you. I'm all you got, boo. You're nothing without me."

I chuckle. "No, you were all I had. It's funny how you have my insecurities memorized while overlooking your own. However, you can rattle off the list of darkness I've endured, and it still doesn't change the fact I'd rather be nothing without you than broken with you. Hold on, how did you know I'm getting baptized?"

"I know everything about you."

"It's apparent you don't." I go over and open the door. "Goodbye Andre and make it for good this time."

He stops in front of me with a smile that sends a chill down my spine.

"I pray you find what you need."

"I already have." He says before grabbing me by the throat with both hands, lifting me from the floor. Dazed, it takes a few seconds before reality kicks in, and I start grabbing at his hands to loosen the grip. I continue to kick the door hearing glass break. He flings me inside, never letting go which causes us both to fall. He lands on top with me clawing at his face and hands. His eyes are full of anger and hatred.

"Do you think I'll let you leave after all I've invested in you? I saved you." He growls, spit dripping onto my face. "You belong to me, and I'd rather watch the life drain from your eyes than to see you with someone else."

I continue to hit and kick, inwardly praying for God to not let me die as my vision becomes blurry. He finally releases me, and I pant and cough trying to catch my breath. I feel him towering over me and I attempt to move when his steel toe boot connects with my rib cage. I roll over, reaching for the coffee table to get up.

I open my mouth to scream, but nothing comes out as he continues to yell. I can't make out what he's saying due to the ringing in my ears. I stagger towards the kitchen to get my phone and he grabs my hair dragging me down the hall. I turn to push him, and he punches me in the face.

chapter twenty-eight
Andre

"Look what you made me do." I slam her down on the bed beginning to pace. "You don't get to decide when this is over. Do you hear me?" I smack her cheek. "How dare you think you can just walk away like what we shared meant nothing. Yes, I made a lot of mistakes but so did you."

"Andre." She moans.

"That's right baby. Andre, not that white boy. You belong to me and after today, you'll know it." I kiss her lips before pushing up her dress and removing her underwear. "You're mine Ava and I want you to have my baby." I tell her while undressing then inserting myself into her. She moans again, tears slipping from her eyes. "I've missed you too baby, but I'm here now." When it's over, I kiss her again before going into the bathroom to turn on the shower.

"Babe— I stop when I hear someone coming into the house.

"Ava, hello. It's Josiah. I'm here to drop off the tile. Ava are you okay?" he yells. "Call out if you're in trouble."

I step into the hall coming face to face with a dude.

"Where's Ava?"

I laugh. "Bro, Ava isn't your concern and whatever y'all had going on is over now since daddy is home."

"I'm going to ask you again. Where's Ava?"

"I must be invisible. I'm giving you three seconds to get out of my house."

"This isn't your house, it's mine."

"Oh, my bad bro. You must be the landlord. What's up I'm Andre, Ava's boyfriend." I extend my hand.

"Where's Ava?" he asks with a little more force looking me up and down.

"She's taking a shower."

"With broken glass and an open door? Can you ask her to come out for a second?" he requests.

"Things heated up rather quickly and she couldn't resist big daddy." I smile rubbing down my chest grabbing my crotch. "I'm sorry about the door, I'll fix it later. Now, if you don't mind, I'd like to finish what we started. I'll have Ava call you whenever we're done."

"As a matter of fact, I do mind." He pulls a gun from his waist. "Memphis Police, show me your hands."

"I'm not showing you shit, and you need to chill man. I'm also an officer and you're the one trespassing."

"Yeah, then arrest me but until Ava appears well and unharmed, you need to show me your hands."

"Rainey, you in here?"

"Yeah, I have one suspect at gunpoint in the hall." He shouts.

"Mane, I know you didn't call the police on me." I laugh as two more officers walk towards us. "Ole shaky ass nigga. You couldn't handle me on your own?" I taunt. "Y'all look like you got more sense than his square head ass. I told him I'm an officer. Andre Powell, 9th Precinct, badge—

"Dude, we don't care. Show your hands."

I put them on my crotch. "See."

"Sir, this is the last time I'm going to ask."

When one of them move towards me, I lunge, dropping when the taser connects with my skin.

"Ah. Aite, aite." I scream.

"Stop moving." They order turning me on my back and applying cuffs.

"Dispatch, we need EMS, crime scene and a commanding officer to our location."

Hours later, I'm dressed in nurses' scrubs with bandages on my face banging on the door of the cold interrogation room.

The door opens. "Dude, sit down and cut out all the noise." A female officer says pushing me into the chair.

I jump up. "Bit—

"Finish it and I'll take the write up for beating you like your mammy should have done. You may get off on beating women, but I promise you, I ain't the one today or tomorrow."

I wave her off. "Girl, gone."

"Typical. You only find your balls to hit somebody you've deemed weaker than you. Insecure boy."

"You want to find out?"

"And do." She replies looking me in the eyes as the door opens and another lady walks in.

"Is everything okay?" she inquires.

"Yes ma'am." The officer answers never taking her eyes off me. "Just handling an unruly perp."

"I got your perp, dude." I mock taking a seat. "Why am I here?"

"Mr. Powell, my name is Captain Angela Wyatt and you're here because of the assault that took place."

"Captain?" I chuckle. "You're a woman."

"Yep, been one for the last fifty-two years. Now, before we proceed—

"Figures they'd send a woman to do a man's job. Well, captain, what can I do for you?"

"If you'd stop interrupting, I can tell you."

I sit back and fold my arms.

"First, I need to cover the preliminaries. Andre Powell, you have the right to remain silent. Anything—

"I know my rights and I don't need you reciting them because I didn't commit a crime."

"You have the right to remain silent sir. Anything you say can and will be used against you in a court of law. You have the right to an attorney. If you cannot afford an attorney, one will be provided for you. Do you understand the rights I have just read to you?"

"Yep."

"With these rights in mind, do you wish to speak to me?" she asks.

"Look," I sit up, "I feel like I'm being harassed. What happened was between me and my girl and y'all are violating my rights."

"And we can talk about that once you've given consent to answer questions without an attorney present." She states. "Would you like to speak to me without an attorney."

"There's nothing to talk about. No crime was committed."

"Mr. Powell."

"Officer. I'm an officer of the law." I strike the table. "Respect me."

She leans back in the chair. "You can continue with the dramatics Mr. Powell, or we can end things. Your choice."

"Either charge me or let me go, Captain."

"Fine. Andre Powell, you're under arrest for aggravated domestic assault and aggravated rape. Please stand."

"Domestic Assault? Rape? How can I rape what belongs to me? Furthermore, are y'all going to charge her for what she did to my face?"

She stands, walking toward the door. "Another officer will be in to transport you to booking."

I angrily push the table away. "Don't walk away from me. I'm an officer of the law and I have rights."

"You have the right to shut up." The other officer laughs, throwing the deuces while closing the door.

chapter twenty-nine
Andre

Two hours later, I'm led to booking where other officers are looking, laughing, and shaking their head.

"What the hell y'all looking at?"

"Andre, man dannggg," he sings. "Bro, what happened to you?"

"Nothing, nosy nigga and I'm not your bro. Do your job and get this over with."

"Say no more inmate." He snatches my arm pushing me into a room.

"You know the drill Powell." Officer Langston Conners says. "I need your legal name, home address, birthdate and a contact person."

"Andre Powell, 5433 Chariot Drive, Memphis, TN 38114. December twelfth, nineteen seventy-seven. Uh, my momma. Charlene Powell. Nine oh one, three seven-seven, nine zero four six."

"Are you currently being treated for any medical or psychological issues?" he asks.

"Nope."

"Any tattoos or gang affiliations?"

I look at him.

"Yes, or no?"

"One tattoo, no gang."

I show him the tattoo and afterwards, he continues with more stupid questions.

"Man, enough of all this. When is pretrial?"

"They'll come get you when it's your turn. Follow me."

After being issued an inmate number, fingerprinted, all my personal items removed, mug shot taken, and given a jumpsuit I'm moved to a separate holding area. Getting to the phone, I dial my mother's number.

"Marble, I need you to come bail me out." I tell her. "It's a long story. Can you do this for me or not? Two days, are you serious? Ma, I can't call Ava. Look, don't worry about it. I'll figure it out." I slam the receiver down.

"Dre, what's up boo. I didn't expect to see you on that side of the wall. You good?"

I look up at Officer Crystal Dunagan. "Does it look like it?"

"No need to get snippy with her, Robocop." Officer Ray Lawrence comes in. "She didn't tell you to go all Kung-Fu panda on some chick."

"Yeah, but did you hear he pissed himself when the taser hit him?" somebody says, and they all laugh.

"Y'all only talking because I'm on this side." I calmly tell them. "Let's meet when I post bail."

"When being the vital word in case your paperwork gets lost, pissy."

"Okay Ray, that's enough." Crystal tells him. "Go on."

She waits until they leave and comes over to me. "Dre, what is wrong with you? I've never seen you like this."

"I'm good, just need to get out of here."

"Pre-trial shouldn't be long after you're processed. Keep your head up."

"Wait. I need a favor." I tell her looking around.

"What's up?"

"Let me use your cell phone."

"You know I can't do that."

"Come on Ma and do me a solid. I'll make it up to you when I'm out."

"Yeah, like calling me back after we hooked up." She rolls her eyes.

"I lost your number."

"Yet you know where I work."

"Please." I beg taking her hand. "I need to make a call I don't want recorded. Babe, come on. I'm tired and in pain. It'll be quick."

She looks around. "Two minutes."

Dialing Ava's number, I move away from her as the phone connects. No one says anything.

"Hello, Ava, are you there?" I exhale. "I know you're mad, but baby I need you. I tried calling my mother to bail me out, but she's out of town and won't be back for two days. Ava, I can't stay here, and I need you to find a bail bondsman and get me out. I don't know how much it'll cost yet, but you'll find a way. You always do. Anyway, once we get home, we'll discuss you not pressing charges. Ava, say something. Babe, I'm not mad because this isn't your fault. It's that nosey landlord of yours. I'll deal with him later."

"Negro, you've lost the last little bit of mind I thought you had. You got the nerve to call this woman's phone whining after what you did. You need to rot in hell."

"Who is this?"

"The person who's going to report you, punk. You tried to kill her and now you think she's going to bail you out."

"Aw, this must be June. Junie girl, you know nothing about us so give Ava the phone and stay out of grown folk business."

"I know she isn't coming to post bond."

"My Ava will do whatever I ask. She always does. Give her the phone."

"She isn't yours anymore, Satan. Don't call this phone again."

"June, don't hang—June!"

"Dude." Dunagan rushes over snatching her phone. "You're going to get me caught with all this screaming. You need to chill."

"I can't stay here Crystal." I tell her. "Can you check and see how much longer it'll be or make sure my paperwork is processed first?"

"I'll see what I can do."

chapter thirty
Ava

"Lord, you're a healer and restorer. Your word says in Jeremiah seventeen and fourteen, "*heal me, o Lord, and I shall be healed; save me, and I shall be saved, for you are my praise.*" Father, heal Ava, o Lord, and she shall be healed. Save Ava, and Ava shall be saved, for you are our praise. Heal, o Lord. In the name of Jesus."

I open my eyes at the sound of someone praying, unsure of where I am.

"Heal in your time God."

With my eyes clearer, I realize it's a hospital. Trying to move causes pain. I moan.

"Hey." I hear someone say. "You're awake."

Turning, I frown confused at the sight of June. I open my mouth, but it's too dry to speak.

"Let me get you some water."

After a few sips, she dabs my mouth with a napkin.

"What happened?" I question clearing my burning throat.

"You were attacked," she pauses, "by Andre but you're going to be fine."

I wince from pain all over, closing my eyes trying to remember.

"What did he do?" I cry.

"You have a few bruised ribs, swelling around your neck and—let me just tell the nurse you're awake and she can call the doctor. He'll explain everything."

"Wait." I bring my hand to my throat. "Did they arrest him?"

"Yes. He's in jail where he belongs. You rest and I'll be back."

I exhale, closing my eyes.

Minutes later, she returns.

"She's paging the doctor."

I swallow as tears fall from the physical and mental pain. "I thought he was going to kill me." I whisper to her.

"Shh." She rubs my forehead. "You're safe now. He's in jail and we're going to make sure he never gets close enough to hurt you again."

"Knock, knock. Ms. Gentry, hi, I'm Dr. Sanford. How are you feeling?"

"Like I've been in a fight and lost."

He lays the tablet beside me on the bed, putting on gloves. When he touches my neck, I cringe.

"You sustained injuries to your throat that's causing the hoarseness of your voice, trouble swallowing and swelling. There's a cut on the bridge of your nose that required a few stitches and in the coming days, you may notice more bruising under your eyes."

"Do you mean I'll have black eyes?"

"Yes. Open for me. You also have what we call petechiae in your mouth and around the eyes. They are small spots caused by bleeding under the skin, due to the excessive pressure you endured. I've started you on corticosteroids to reduce swelling in the blood vessels and you'll go home with a prescription."

He moves down to my ribs.

"Oh." I cry out when he touches me.

"You also have some bruised ribs on your right side. Although they are painful, rest along with ice packs and naproxen will help them to heal within four to six weeks. I'd like to get an MRI of your head, to rule out concussion and other injuries. However, before we do that, we need to perform a rape kit."

I look at him with confusion.

"Rape?"

June squeezes my hand.

"He raped me. Oh, my God."

"Ms. Gentry, I know you've been through a lot and it's up to you whether to go through with the medical exam. However, it will help with ensuring your attacker is punished for his actions."

"Can I be with her?" June asks.

"Unfortunately, not during the exam."

"It's okay." I tell June. "I'll do it." I say to the doctor. He looks back at the nurse standing near the door.

"The exam should take about an hour. Once we're done, the nurse will come and get you." He tells June.

"I'll be right outside." June assures me.

"Ms. Gentry, my name is Charlotte and I'll be with you every step of the way. I won't lie, this will be uncomfortable, but we'll move as fast as possible to get it done. Also, I'll explain everything we do and if you choose to decline any part, it's your choice. If you're ready, sign here."

Sixty-two minutes later, I'm on my back staring at the ceiling, feeling violated all over again. Every inch of my body has been photographed, swabbed, scraped, combed over, and investigated. The worst part, having to take a Plan B and medications to prevent STDs because the man I've spent the last thirteen years with raped me.

I jump when I feel someone touch me.

"It's just me." June says. "Is there anything you need?"

"To rewind time. June, why would he do this? I knew he didn't love me, but I never thought he'd do this." I burst into tears and can't tell if the majority of the pain is coming from my injuries or my heart. "It hurts."

"You've been through something no one would wish on their enemy, by the hands of a man you once trusted. Ava, you're going to hurt, be angry, question why this, and why you all while healing. Will it get easier? Yes, in due time but you have to make it to see that time. For now, you don't need permission to cry. You have that right."

She slowly climbs into the bed with me.

"Thank you for being here and I'm sorry you're having to deal with this. I don't even know how they knew to call you, but I'm glad they did."

"Remember when you sprained your ankle at the company retreat last year? You listed me as an emergency contact, and I guess it was never changed. However, I'm also here because that's what friends do."

Someone taps on the door. "Hi, my apology for intruding. My name is Detective Maurice Faison and my partner, Detective Jason Turnage. May we ask you a few questions."

chapter thirty-one

"Sure." June motions for them to come in while getting up.

"Please stay." I tell her. "This is my friend, June Carson."

"Is it okay if I record this?" one of them asks.

"Yes."

"Sunday, September 26, 2021, 11:25 PM. In the room are Detective Maurice Faison, Detective Jason Turnage, Ava Gentry and June Carson. Ms. Gentry, can you tell me how you know Andre Powell?" he inquires standing at the foot of the bed.

"We've been in a relationship for over thirteen years."

"Has he ever been violent towards you before today?"

"Not physically."

"In what other ways?" he questions.

"Let's just say, he has a way with words."

"Got it." He makes some notes.

"Wait, who called the police?" I question.

"Officer Josiah Rainey. We've learned he's your landlord who came by to drop off tile and found the door busted."

"Yes, I've been renting from him for a few months."

"Ms. Gentry, can you walk us through what happened earlier today?" the other detective asks.

"I came in from church and Andre was already there."

"Did you give him a key?" he interrupts.

"Hell no." I wince from the pain. "He had no reason to have a key to my home because we are no longer together. I don't know how he got in. Anyway, he started going on about how he'd given me time to come to my senses and come back to him. When I refused and asked him to leave, he attacked me. I tried to fight him off, but he was too strong. It was like he turned into someone else. I thought I was going to die."

June touches my hand.

"So, he went from zero to one hundred because you refused to take him back? Is that all?"

"What are you insinuating?" June asks him. "People kill for less than that."

"I thought my questioning was clear ma'am. Did anything else happen to cause him to react like he did?"

"Are you asking what I did to deserve this?" I question.

"I'm only asking to ensure we get all the facts. Are you seeing someone else?" Detective Turnage inquires. "Is that why he attacked you, he caught you cheating?"

"Are you serious?" June steps in. "Cheating insinuates a relationship and there isn't one, she told you that. Besides, he was in her home, unauthorized."

"People lie ma'am."

"I don't give a flying flip of a blueberry pancake if she is or isn't lying or whether she is or isn't seeing somebody else. It didn't give him a right to put his hands around her throat. See, people like you are part of the problem when it comes to domestic violence. Abuse victims have to deal with mess like this from men like you who probably got mommy issues and don't know how to treat a woman. You show up in times like this judging the victim when it's your job to serve and protect."

"I'm only trying to get both sides of the story." He counters. "And I don't have mommy issues, this is called doing my job."

"Then you need better training." June retorts.

"Ma'am, that's not what I'm doing. It's our job to investigate claims of this matter because women have been known to make accusations and then drop the charges. We have a lot of other cases to tend too and if Ms. Gentry isn't going to follow through, it'll save us a lot of time."

"You're an arrogant son-of-a-female dog." June bellows. "I pray you never get a call from a woman in your family who's been victimized because I'd hate for her to need you in her time of need."

"Turnage, how about you let me finish this." Detective Faison states looking at him.

"Nah, I'm good." He replies scribbling in his notebook.

"It wasn't a request. Wait outside."

"Hope you feel better ma'am." He smirks walking out.

"Ms. Gentry, please accept my apology on behalf of my partner. I don't condone his line of questioning or attitude. I can assure you this case will be treated like any other and I'm going to do everything I can to ensure the perpetrator of this crime will be punished."

"Thank you."

"That's all well and good," June cuts in, "but what are y'all doing to make sure he doesn't come back."

"He isn't going to get bail, is he?" I ask.

"That'll be up to the judge."

"How can she get an order of protection because he called her phone earlier and I need to make sure he can't come anywhere near her." June inquires.

"When?" we both ask at the same time.

"A couple hours ago. It was from an unsaved number and since he's supposed to be in jail, I can assume it wasn't his phone. Nonetheless, he was begging Ava to bail him out. He didn't know it was me who answered."

"Do you have the number he called from?"

June hands me the phone, I unlock it for him to make note of the number.

"Thanks. Here's information for the Shelby County Rape Crisis Center. They can help you get an order of protection. However, even if you choose to get one, the judge will usually issue no contact orders as bail conditions with assault cases."

I nod.

"I'll let you rest. Will it be okay to contact you in a few days to follow up?"

"Sure, only if the other detective isn't with you. I plan on getting a hotel   room—

"You're coming home with me." June cuts in.

"I can't impose on you and Grant."

"You're not imposing and I'm not taking no for an answer. Detective Faison, let me give you my address as Ava will be with us until she's ready to go home."

"Thank you. Get some rest. If you have questions or need anything from me, don't hesitate to call."

chapter thirty-two

Standing in the bathroom mirror of June's guestroom, after a shower, I rub over the bruises on my neck and face.

"They'll heal."

I'm startled by the sound of June's voice.

"I'm sorry, didn't mean to scare you. I brought you juice to take your meds and to see if you need help getting dressed."

I let my arms fall to my side.

"Ava, what is it?"

"When I was little, I'd stand on a stool in the mirror, like this, after being abused by my grandfather. He'd grip me so tight; the outline of his fingers would be embedded in my skin. I would stay there for the longest trying to understand what I did to make him hate me as much as he did. It didn't matter how good my grades were, how well I cleaned the house or how quiet I stayed, he'd still find a reason to inflict pain. Not ordinary pain though. No." I shake my head. "He'd impose the kind that made it hurt to inhale and he'd do it with this look in his eyes, as if he was a different person. Yet, even knowing he was a monster, I still kicked and screamed when CPS came to take me away."

"You were a child being removed from the only home you knew." She says with tears falling.

"I thought so too until a psychology professor, in college, talked about this thing called a trauma bond."

"I've never heard of it."

"It's when you connect with your abuser. Research says it happens when the abused begins to feel sympathy or affection for the abuser."

"Oh, like Stockholm Syndrome?"

"Yeah. It took me years to realize, my pleas for my grandfather weren't out of love. They came from the bond of abuse that attached us. You know what I realized tonight?"

"What?" she replies.

"Andre is a version of my grandfather and because I never destroyed the bond, I simply attached myself to someone who picked up where he left off." I turn back to the mirror. "I'm still that scared eight-year-old girl yearning for love even if it has to hurt."

"Ava, love isn't supposed to hurt. You know that right?"

"I wish I did." I honestly answer. "It's all I've ever known."

"Well, it doesn't have to be going forward. Ava, it may not seem like it now, but the blessing in what you've experienced is the fact you survived and now have the opportunity to destroy the bond trauma created, once and for all."

"How?" I ask her.

"Girl, I don't know, but I'll move mountains to find someone who can tell you." She smiles. "Ava, you've already endured the worst parts of life, how about we get you healed in order to see what's on the other side."

"If I wasn't hurting, I'd give you the biggest hug. Thank you for all you've done June. I truly appreciate it."

"It's okay, I'll take a hug raincheck to be redeemed once you're healed. Now, come let's get you to bed. It's been a long day."

June's husband, Grant was able to meet Josiah at the house to get a few things I jotted down, including my laptop. Taking the pain meds, I settle in the bed and open the computer to see it's after five in the morning. Opening Google, I type Andre's name.

Nothing comes up. I try the news website.

"Memphis police officer charged with aggravated rape." I read before clicking on the article.

A MPD officer has been relieved of duty after police say he was involved in a domestic altercation. Sources within the department won't tell us the officer's name, but we know he's been charged with Aggravated Domestic Assault and Aggravated Rape after assaulting an unknown female victim. Although police have not released details, we have learned the officer has been relieved of duty with pay pending the outcome of the investigation and will face a judge on Monday for arraignment.

Clicking in the search bar, I type, 'order of protection Memphis.' Clicking on the crime victim center's website, I read through the information before filling out the online application. Done, I close the laptop, push it off my lap and struggle to get comfortable.

Getting my phone, I see the missed calls and texts from Katrina. I make a mental note to call her in the morning before dialing Josiah's number putting it on speaker.

"Ava." He answers groggily. "Are you okay?"

"No." I cry. "I'm sorry to wake you."

"It's okay, we've been waiting to hear from you. Is there anything we can do for you?"

"The door, I think I broke the glass in it. I will get someone to fix it and pay for whatever damage."

"Don't worry about that. Grant and I was able to get it repaired and everything locked up when he came by earlier. All you need to do is focus on getting better. He told me you're staying with him and his wife June."

"Yeah." I sigh. "Josiah, I'm sorry for bringing this drama to your house. I'll understand if you want to terminate the lease."

"Ava, stop. This isn't on you. Your lease is still good. However, I am having the locks changed, adding motion lights and an alarm panel. I also fixed the back door which is how I believe your attacker was able to get in, but we can talk about this later. Get some rest."

"I don't think I'll be able to sleep."

"Dear God, I pray in this hour you'll grant sleep to my sister Ava. Father, not just any sleep but peaceful rest. God, you know what she's gone through, don't allow the enemy to interrupt her thoughts by replaying it. Comfort her mind while healing her inside and out. Surround her in the safety of heaven's angels so that no further hurt or harm shall come her way. Send peace now, God that will allow her to sleep like Daniel did in the lion's den. This I pray, in the name of Jesus. Amen."

"Amen. Thank you for everything."

"No problem. Goodnight, rather good morning. We'll talk soon."

Pressing the phone against my chest, it vibrates. Looking at the screen, it's an unknown caller and against my better judgement, I answer it.

"Hello."

"Hello, my name is Sherman from In and Out Bail, trying to reach Ava Gentry."

"Speaking."

"Ms. Gentry, I'm calling on behalf of Andre Powell."

"Sir, let me stop you. I'm not interested in anything regarding him. Please remove my name and number as a method of contact."

"Oh, I, well ma'am, I'm not calling for money. His lawyer states he has the money, but he needs someone to sign the paperwork and he gave your name."

"Mr. Sherman, I don't care if he gave you the name above all names. I'm not signing anything for him." I wince trying not to breathe or talk too hard. "Sir, Andre is in jail for attacking me. At this very moment, I can't even get comfortable enough to sleep because of pain from the bruised ribs he left me with. My face and neck are covered in bruises caused by him wrapping his hands around my neck. Oh, shall I also give details of how he raped me while I was unconscious or not?"

"I wasn't aware, I'm sorry." He somberly says.

"So am I. Sorry for meeting a piece of garbage like Andre. So, please let him and his lawyer know I wouldn't sign a piece of paper to give him a drink of water, let alone bail. Oh, and while you're at it, give him a message."

"Okay."

"Let them know I said, f them and Sherman, remove my name and number."

"Yes ma'am."

I drop the phone onto the bed. "He got the nerve to think I'll bail him out of jail after what he did—ah." I groan sliding under the comforter angry at myself for letting things get this bad. I knew better than to stay. "God, if you happen to hear this message while searching through the backlog of sinner's prayers, please know I can't do this on my own. I know I've had you on hold for a long time, but I need you. Please see about me." I yawn.

chapter thirty-three

Look what you made me do. You don't get to decide when this is over. Do you hear me? How dare you think you can just walk away like what we shared meant nothing. Yes, I made a lot of mistakes but so did you.

My eyes fly open as the sound of thunder rattles the windows. Touching my chest, I feel the rapid beating of my heart. "He's not here." I repeat to calm myself while looking over at the clock. 7:09 AM. "You will no longer disturb my peace."

I lay there allowing the tears to fall with the rain.

*****

"Ava. Hey Ava, have you heard anything I said?" Dorothy from the Shelby County Crime Victims and Rape Crisis Center asks touching my arm which causes me to jump.

"Huh?" I reply looking around.

"He's not here Ava."

"I know." I sigh. "It feels like he'll come around the corner at any moment."

"Even if he does, the judge has ordered him to have no contact with you in any form. This means in person, text, email, or smoke signal. Neither can he make or commit any threats of violence or have any guns." She tells me.

"Yeah, it doesn't mean he'll comply."

"He has no choice. Your court date has been set for October 12th. At that time you'll need a lawyer because this is the time for Andre to make his appeal to the court as to why the order shouldn't be extended. In the meantime, he'll be served the temporary order. If he violates any part, call 911 immediately. Do you understand?"

I nod.

"Ava, abusers are conning and will do whatever they can to get you to drop the charges. I know you've been in a long-term relationship with Mr. Powell, but do not entertain any conversation with him in public or private. If there's anything that needs to be discussed, do it at your lawyer's office."

"I understand."

"Good. You have my card as well as the information for the domestic violence group which meets on Thursdays. You're more than welcome to join us. Call me if there's anything you need."

"I'll be fine."

"Yeah, you will be, but you aren't right now. Don't for a second think it's easier to keep things bottled up because the enemy will use the silence to speak to you. Give your pain a voice or the pain can try to take yours. Ava, you've gone through a traumatic ordeal, you don't have to be strong."

"Thank you." I tell her.

"How did it go?" June asks when I get inside the car.

"The judge issued a temporary order, but we have to go back to have it extended permanently. The courts have to give Andre a chance to defend himself. It's not like my body isn't covered in bruises and he was found standing over me. He still has to defend my ask for a protection order. Isn't that crazy? Your abuser gets the opportunity to defend himself on why you shouldn't be ordered to stay away from the person he kicked like a discarded drink can."

"Ava."

"I know June." I snap at her before exhaling. "I'm sorry. What if he gets away with this?"

"No. Don't do that. Andre will pay for what he did."

"He's the police." I tell her.

"Yeah, but he isn't above the law."

"I wish I had your confidence."

"Well sis, I have enough for the both of us."

She pats my leg, putting the car in drive as I lean my head against the headrest. Feeling someone touching me, I jerk.

"Ah." I groan from moving too fast.

"Ava, you're okay. We're home."

I look around, not realizing I'd fallen asleep.

"I'm sorry." I yawn. "I haven't been sleeping well."

"I understand. Come on. You can take a nap while I fix lunch."

"June, thank you." I tell her when we make it inside. "I didn't mean to disrupt your life with all my drama."

"You aren't. I'm here because I love you and you shouldn't have to deal with everything by yourself. And Ava."

"Yeah."

"Stop apologizing."

I nod, grabbing a bottle of water from the refrigerator and heading into the living room to see the TV is paused on yesterday's service from June's church.

"She had a great message." June states. "Listen to it."

I rewind part ways then click play on the remote.

"Witnessing abuse is traumatic. The other thing is childhood, religious, medical, and financial trauma, along with neglect, torture, bullying, infidelity, harassment, homelessness, and the list goes on and on. All those things can cause complex post-traumatic stress disorder and when you have CPTSD, it causes you to do things. You'll have the core PTSD symptoms, but you'll also have difficulty controlling your emotions. You'll have low self-esteem, difficulty with relationships, loss of core beliefs, and detachment from trauma. You ever met somebody who was just numb? David, Saul tried to kill you twice and you still stay connected to him? Numb. So, there are lasting impressions from being picked last.

David was picked last, but not just from anybody He was picked last by his daddy. Some of y'all ain't even been picked by your daddy and that hurts worse. If you're just tuning in, my name is Dr. Kia Moore, pastor of the Church at the Well in Memphis, TN. We're concluding our series on self-love with a discussion about David's childhood trauma, David's pain, David's wounds and how we can see ourselves in David. He was anointed, no doubt, being used by God, had a purpose and a promise, but he'd gone through so much that it was influencing, I argue today, his decision making. Ask yourself the question, how much of David do I have in me.

The first thing God began to show me as I walked through this text, looking at what other people had been saying about the trajectory of David's life and how his worst moments were colored by his first worst moments.

The first thing I began to see is, if you struggle with loving yourself and seeing your true worth, it's because you've got wounds from being picked last, rejected, hurt, overlooked, neglected, or abused. And a lot of you don't realize you're struggling with these things because you don't know what neglect is. When they ghosted you, they neglected you and it's caused some of you to have PTSD. That's why, the first thing God showed me was, you make decisions that don't reflect self-care."

I pause the TV. "Wow."

"It's heavy right?" June asks coming in with a glass of strawberry lemonade. "It fits with what you were talking about, the trauma bonds. She said being rejected as a child can color your relationships with toxic people and shapes your ability to make decisions. It also influences you to stay in bad situations and connected to the wrong people even when God has given you an out, an opportunity to exit or do better."

"I know, okay. You don't have to keep saying it. I get it. I messed up. I should have left sooner and maybe I wouldn't be going through any of this."

She sits beside me. "Ava, stop. I'm not judging you."

"You don't have too." I angrily swipe the tears from my face. "I'm doing enough of it myself. June, why was I so stupid to think Andre could be what I needed? He's never shown me an ounce of compassion or love yet, I stayed. Why?"

"Aw sweetie." She grabs my hand. "You know why you stayed, so don't keep questioning the why when you are way past that. Your focus should be on what's next because it's harder to move forward than backwards. Lunch will be ready in an hour. Try to rest."

When she walks away, I realize she's right. I stayed because it was easier than starting over even though staying was destroying me. I get the remote before propping a pillow on my right side as I attempt to get comfortable on the couch. Pressing play, I slowly lay back, closing my eyes.

"Who am I talking too? You're powerful, smart, and anointed but keep finding yourself pinned up against the wall brokenhearted, neglected, left for dead, ignored, and abandoned. There's something going on, in your mind, that makes you loyal to things that are not loyal to you. People who have not cared for themselves will have their backs against the wall and still choose the wrong person. Why didn't David leave the first time Saul tried to kill him?"

I cover my face as tears spill from my eyes.

"Why didn't he leave the second time?" pastor Moore continues. "Let me help you see something. A lot of us struggle because we want to see the good in people when they've already shown us who they are."

chapter thirty-four
Andre

Walking into the administrative offices of the police department, I see Crystal coming towards me. Getting closer, she shoves me.

"What is wrong with you? I told you I'll call when I get this mess straightened out. Chill."

"Forget that. I can lose my job." She yells.

"What did you do?"

"Helped you. You smug bastard."

"Oh."

"Oh. Is that all you're going to say? My commander found out I let you use my phone, to call the woman you're accused of attacking. Why would you put me in the middle of this?"

"Crystal, I'm sorry, but it's not that big of a deal. You're a woman, think of a good lie. That's something y'all are good at. Tell them I took the phone when you weren't looking or something."

"Lie?" she chuckles. "You want me to lie when I'm already facing possible criminal charges and the loss of my job?"

"Crystal, you need to chill. You didn't do anything to warrant criminal charges. I used your phone, big freaking deal. It's not like I talked to Ava anyway. Her friend was the one who answered the phone."

"You don't get how bad this is. I need this job."

"Then all I can tell you to do is fight for it. I got to go. Good luck."

"Andre." I hear her yell.

I take the stairs to the 3rd floor.

"Office Powell, you may go in." The young lady tells me.

I push open the door to see Chief Rodney Lomax, Deputy Chief Uniform Patrol Samuel Oakley, Internal Affairs Rep and a few more people I didn't know.

"Officer Powell, please have a seat. You are aware of your right to have representation present for this meeting, right?"

"Yes, but it's not needed. I know how this goes."

"Very well. On Sunday, September 26, 2021, you were arrested for aggravated domestic assault and rape. Under policy, you are required to submit a written memo immediately when you are arrested for any misdemeanor or felony offense. As of today, it has not been done."

"I'm aware, and I didn't intentionally overlook it, but I had more pressing matters to attend to, like bailing out of jail on these bogus charges."

"We are not here to attest to the validity of your charges. The purpose of this meeting is to officially relieve you of your duties as a Memphis Police Department officer in pursuant to the policies and procedures you vowed to when you were sworn in." Chief Lomax advises.

"Couldn't this have been done over the phone?" I ask standing up throwing my badge on the desk and removing my weapon. "What happened to innocent until proven guilty? Isn't there supposed to be an investigation?"

Deputy Chief Oakley stands, sliding the paperwork across the table.

I look through it to see the arresting reports, pictures, and statements before pushing it away.

"Officer Powell, as your superior officer, I speak for the department when I tell you how disappointed we are in your actions. You've served this community for over fifteen years, and we hate it had to end like this, yet you left us no choice." He asserts.

"And due to violations of the code of ethics, personal conduct, compliance with regulations, and adherence to law, we hereby revoke your privileges as a police officer and strip you of your state law enforcement certification. While we thank you for the years of service, we cannot have an officer of your caliber representing our city. Your actions were deplorable and go against everything we stand for. Therefore, you are dismissed." Chief Lomax states.

"I've given my life to this police department and y'all dismiss me the first time I make a mistake. Oakley is an alcoholic who like underage girls, Rogers from IAB has had over three DUIs and chief, you can't even control your own wife yet y'all pass judgment on me."

"Sir, you're skating on thin ice."

"Besides, we all know this isn't the first time you've made a mistake. Dude, your file is thicker than an encyclopedia and each of those you've mentioned are the same ones who've covered for you more times than we should."

"So, how about you leave now and save the little dignity you have left." Chief says standing.

"Screw y'all and this job." I kick a chair on my way out.

Hours and a whole lot of liquor later, I'm yelling at the bartender for another drink.

"You've reached your limit my friend." She says removing the empty glass and giving me back my card. "In liquor and finances. Your card was declined."

"Try it again and give me another drink."

"Sir, I'm going to need another card or cash to close out this tab."

"No." I hit the bar. "You need to do your job and get me another got damn drink."

She motions for someone over my shoulder.

"Good. I hope you're calling somebody with better sense of doing their job."

"Sir."

I turn, look over my shoulder and laugh.

"What is she supposed to do?" I refer to the security guard.

"Pay the lady and get out of here. We're not asking again." She emphasizes.

"We're not asking again." I mock.

She grabs my arm and I swing at her. She pins me against the bar with one hand behind my back. Pushing her away, I throw another punch.

*****

"Dude. Hey, dude. They're calling you."

I open my eyes and push him away. "Who are you?"

"Your fairy god-daddy." The dude states before laying back down. "Now, get up so they can shut up." He points.

I blink a few times to clear my vision realizing I'm in jail. Sitting fully up, I rest my throbbing head in my hands.

"Powell, move it." Someone yells.

I stand, stumbling back onto the hard bench hitting my hand, letting out a flurry of curse words. Making it to the door, the jailer grabs my arm dragging me down the corridor.

"Sign out and pick up your personal items."

Walking out I see Langston.

"Dude. What were you thinking?" he starts in. "You could have been charged with another assault had the security guard pressed charges."

"What security guard?"

He scoffs. "You don't remember?"

I shake my head.

"You caused a scene at Bar 6 last night. They called me because I was the last number in your phone, but by the time I got there the police had already taken you away because you kept trying to fight. Oh, I paid your tab. How does one person run up over one hundred dollars drinking?"

"It's easy when you're trying to drown your sorrows. Look Lang, thank you for coming last night and this morning, but can we save the lecture. My head is killing me, and I think I broke my finger."

"That ain't the only thing broke. Here." He hands me my bank card. "Your card was declined."

I get into the passenger seat of his car.

"What's today?" I ask.

"October second."

"The mortgage payment came out. Ava normally took care of the bills and since—I'll pay you back. Let me move some stuff around. In the meantime, can you take me to the emergency room."

chapter thirty-five
Dr. Greene

I walk into my office to see Ava staring ahead. I call her name twice before going over to touch her knee. She jumps.

"Whoa." I take a step back. "Ava, what's going on? Are you okay?"

She chuckles then groans. "Am I okay? How in the hell am I supposed to be okay when it feels like I'm drowning?"

"What's causing you to feel like this because things were getting better in our last sessions?"

"Life." She angrily replies grabbing her side and exhaling. "It's as if I keep being pulled down by something that has ahold of me and no matter what I do, it won't let me go. The more I kick against it, the tighter the hold becomes. I'm at a point where I don't have any more strength to fight." She answers in between small, shallow breaths as tears fall.

"Are you thinking of harming yourself?" I question.

She looks away.

"Ava, are you suicidal?" I ask forcibly.

"No. I just want it to stop."

"You want what to stop?"

"This pain, the nightmares, the thoughts—all of it."

"How long have you been having nightmares?"

"I used to have them when I was removed from my grandfather's house then they stopped."

"Until?"

"Until I was attacked and raped by the man, I've spent the last thirteen years of my life with." I remove the scarf from my neck and sunglasses. "It's taking me a while to answer because of the bruised ribs. Dr. Greene, I knew Andre didn't love me. Truth is, I don't think he's capable of it and while he could get verbally abusive, him wrapping his hands around my throat never crossed my mind as something he'd do. Yet, he did and now I can't even close my eyes without seeing the look in his while he tried to kill me. I keep replaying it over and over."

"That's not uncommon when you've been victimized."

"Please don't call me that." She angrily responds through breaths. "He's already taken my ability to sleep, it hurts to breathe, and I'm scared to go home. Dr. Greene, I'm not a victim. I'm mad."

"Ava, what you're experiencing is called Complex PTSD. A condition that causes you to experience symptoms of Post-Traumatic Stress Disorder along with difficulty controlling your emotions, feeling angry or distrustful."

"It's the second time I've heard this term and it describes my entire life. I just don't get how all this bad stuff can happen to one person. I know I haven't been the best, but why can't I seem to get away from trouble?"

"Have you ever heard of an intimacy stalker?"

She shakes her head.

"It's someone who stalks another because they're delusional, believing the person loves or will love them. Most times, it begins when the relationship ends. The stalker becomes borderline obsessed, their mind convincing them this is their ideal mate."

"Are you saying Andre is stalking me?"

"Not only Andre, but the enemy too. Think about it. For the last few months you've begun building a relationship with God which means ending the relationship with Satan. Satan, a being who attaches himself to the vulnerable, wounded, broken, hopeless, and unloved. As long as you're connected to him, he has no reason to stalk because he believes you to be his. It's not until he recognizes you've woken up to see who you can be without him and moved on. Now, he'll do anything in his power to stake his claim even if that means making your life miserable."

She sobs, taking short breaths.

"How do I survive this?" she gets out.

"I surmise you've gotten an order of protection against Andre and pursuing legal matters, right?"

She nods.

"Do the same against the enemy." I open the Bible app on my iPad. "The Bible tells us in Psalm ninety-one, "He who dwells in the secret place of the Most High shall abide under the shadow of the Almighty. I will say of the Lord, "He is my refuge and my fortress; My God, in Him I will trust." Surely, He shall deliver you from the snare of the fowler and from the perilous pestilence. He shall cover you with His feathers, and under His wings you shall take refuge; His truth shall be your shield and buckler. You shall not be afraid of the terror by night, nor of the arrow that flies by day, nor of the pestilence that walks in darkness, nor of the destruction that lays waste at noonday." Ava, petition God for the protection you need, and He'll give it."

"How?"

"By first recognizing what you're about to ask, you can't do on your own. Second, make an earnest, humble and specific plea to God. Tell God exactly what you need and that you cannot accomplish it without Him. Third, hold God to His word because He is a man who does not lie. Tell Him, Father, your word says in Philippians four and nineteen you'll supply all of my needs according to your riches in glory by Christ Jesus and right now, I need safety, peace, healing, love, and light. God, you are my shepherd, and your sheep is wounded. God, you said I can ask for anything in your name and you'll grant it."

"Lord, I need you." She whispers, slowly inhaling as her leg shakes. "I'm injured, heal me. I'm hurting, help me. Please hear me."

I pour some oil into my hands and go over to sit beside her, taking her hands into mine as she rocks back and forth.

"Abba, I petition your throne calling on the name of Jehovah Rapha to come into this place. Father, I don't need you to simply show up, I need you to shift the atmosphere for Ava Gentry. The Ava Gentry whose been fighting to survive from the moment she was born into the world. The Ava Gentry whose been searching for light in darkness. The Ava Gentry whose yet to find love that doesn't hurt. The Ava Gentry whose seeking you. Come into this place God and let your spirit fall until there's nothing left but you. In the name of Jesus, I ask you to calm Ava's fears, let Ava sleep, give Ava strength. Send confusion to Ava's enemies and heal Ava's wounds. In the name of Jesus, I call forth the Angels of Heaven to surround Ava, protecting her as she comes and goes. The enemy may have begun to attack, but he won't win. The enemy may have used her ex, but God you have the last say. In the name of Jesus, we declare your will to be done. God, you are in control, and we trust you with all things. By faith, I submit this prayer on Ava's behalf believing it's already being worked in her favor. Amen."

chapter thirty-six

Two days later, June pulls into the driveway of my house. I sigh staring out the windshield.

"Are you sure about this? I don't mind coming inside with you."

"No." I smile. "But I need to do this on my own. I've allowed Andre to take a lot of things from me, this space won't be one of them."

She squeezes my hand. "I'm proud of you, however if you change your mind, call. I don't care what time it is."

"I don't know how I'd survive this without you."

"And you never have to find out. I love you." She assures me.

"I love you too."

I get out, punching in the code to open the garage. I wave at June and go inside, pressing the button to close it. There's an envelope taped to the door with the words, new keys, written across the front. I take it off and with my hand on the handle of the door, my heart is nervously beating as I turn it to go in. Walking into the kitchen, I drop my bag and stand there a few seconds before slowly making my way into the living room. I exhale when it's empty and burst into tears. Things are still out of place from the police being there. I rub my hand over some fingerprint dust left on the wall.

Going into the bedroom, I stop in my tracks when I see Andre's shoes and clothes on the floor beside the bed. I fall to my knees, knowing this is where he violated me. I lean over wrapping my arms around my waist, screaming with all the strength I can muster as pain courses through my body.

"You didn't have to do this." I yell. "Lord, help me."

I stay on my knees for as long as I can before it begins to hurt worse. Getting up, I scream while snatching the covers from the bed. Wrapping his clothes in them, I head to the garbage outside. "You no longer have power over me."

Back inside, I take a moment to catch my breath. Going into the pantry, I get the bottle of olive oil and lift it in the air. "God, in my hands this is just a bottle of oil, but I stand asking you to anoint it with power to cleanse my house. In my hands, it can only be used for what it was made for, yet by your power it can sanctify this space. In my hands, it's just oil, but if you breathe on it, God, it becomes holy. I declare it so, in the name of Jesus for today, I'm snatching my life from the hands of evil enemies. I will not be held bound by fear in my own home. You tried devil, but I decree in the name of Jesus, you've got to flee."

I begin to walk around touching the doorknobs and window seals. "Father, I ask you into my home to cover every entrance and exit, every doorpost, threshold, window, air vent or space that can be entered. Saturate this place with your spirit that it scares off any presence of darkness and evil. Cover every inch of this place from ceiling to floor, wall to wall and property line. Father, fill this house with so much of you that it'll be felt long after I'm gone. Fear shall not reside here any longer." I rub my hand over my pillows and bed. "I will sleep peacefully from this day forward. I will know what it feels like to rest. I will know what it's like to be happy. I will know what it's like to be loved. I renounce fear and replace it with the favor of you God who loves me enough to spare my life. I come out of agreement with brokenness, low self-esteem, and doubt, replacing them with love, worthiness and confidence to believe in me."

I walk into the bathroom, stopping at the mirror briefly cringing at the darkened circles under my eyes. Shaking my head, I place my oily hand against it. "I am enough. I am blessed because I believe everything the Lord has said concerning me. I am strong, anointed, gifted and alive. I'm not abandoned nor destroyed. I am healed. The black eyes don't stop me from seeing. The bruised ribs don't prevent me from breathing. The scars don't define who I am. The rape won't ruin me, and the abuse no longer binds me to my past."

I rub oil over my wrists. "I declare the spiritual handcuffs of my past are destroyed and I'm free. Momma, grandma, granddaddy, I forgive you. All of the wicked foster parents, I forgive you. Jack Kingston, I forgive you. Andre Powell, I forgive you. Brokenness, I forgive you. Abuse, I forgive you. Ava, I forgive you. Amen."

Hours and two Naproxen later, I'm on the couch, tired, hurting, and sore after cleaning the entire house. I text June to let her know I'm going to stay here tonight and not to worry. I made sure all of the doors are locked and the lights off as I watch the flicker of the candles from the mantle while listening to Free by Fantasia. The music changes to New Life by John P. Kee.

Oh what a change has come over me. My life has detoured, a life of misery. From darkness you gave me light. All the wrong in my life, you came and made it right. Jesus has given us new life. He has given us new life.

*****

The sound of the doorbell startles me. I quickly sit up, regretting it when the bruised ribs remind me of their existence.

The doorbell rings again.

"Hold on." I breathe out reaching for my phone that's dead on the coffee table. Slowly getting up, I look out of window and scoff.

"You've got to be kidding me. Dude, get off my porch."

"Ava, please give me a minute. I know I shouldn't be here, and you have every right to hate me for what I did to you. I'm sorry. I allowed the emotion of the situation to overshadow moral thinking." He sighs. "I made things worse, never stopping to consider your feelings. I only hope you'll forgive me and—

I shake my head, walking away from the door and Jack and into my bathroom to take a shower. Afterwards, I get my phone off the charger to see a text message from June.

June: Good morning sister. You're stronger than you know, and I pray you were able to rest last night. Let me know you're okay.

Me: Good morning and I did. I fell asleep on the couch. LOL. Yet, I feel good this morning and you're absolutely right. I am strong. I'll be by later. I have to order new bedding. #explainlater

Laying the phone down, I remember I need to call Katrina. Picking it back up, I call but she doesn't answer.

Katrina: Hey, sorry I've been MIA. Call me when you get a chance.

Getting my laptop from the bag on the kitchen counter, I plug it in while preparing a cup of coffee and scrambled eggs. Sitting at the island, I search JCP for new bedding. When the order is complete, I call the alarm company and schedule them to come out tomorrow to activate the system. Afterwards, I dial Josiah's number, pressing the speaker button and laying it on the counter.

"Ava, hey. How are you?" he answers.

"I'm getting better. Josiah, I can't thank you enough for everything you've done and for saving my life. God only knows what could have happened had you not showed up when you did."

"We won't even think about that. I'm simply grateful God allowed me to be there and for sparing your life."

"Me too."

"Were you able to get the new alarm set?" he asks.

"I called and scheduled them to come out tomorrow, but I wanted to make sure you and Naomi are truly okay with me staying. I'll understand if you want to terminate the lease."

"What happened wasn't your fault and Naomi and I understand that."

"He's right." I hear Naomi in the background. "Your lease is still in effect unless you need to break it, then we'd understand."

"No." I answer quickly. "For the first time, I feel like I'm home and I'm not going to allow evil to take it from me."

"Then it's settled."

"Ava, I've never been in your shoes, so I cannot begin to understand how you're feeling. However, I know what it's like to feel safe in your own home. If staying there does that for you, stay. We're just thankful to God you're okay." Naomi says. "And we mean it when we say to call if there's anything you need. I don't know why God allowed our paths to cross, yet I've got to believe it's for a purpose."

"Thank you and I will."

When we hang up, I pray God repays their faithfulness.

chapter thirty-seven
Andre

I walk into the office of my lawyer, Langston Abernathy. He holds up a finger then points to the Air Pod in his ear.

"Come on man, I know you can do better. He's been a cop in this city for over fifteen years. I—I, yes, I get that. No—fine, I'll talk to him and get back to you."

He looks at his phone then at me.

"Have a seat. We have about thirty minutes before we need to walk over to the courthouse to deal with the order of protection. How's the hand?"

"It's fine. Who was that?"

"The assistant district attorney."

I shake my head. "I'm not taking a plea. I told you to let me talk to Ava. I know I can get her to drop the charges."

"Ava isn't an option and don't you dare try to contact her. As conditions of your bail, you can't, or you risk it being revoked."

"Man, y'all treating her like she's a victim."

"Do you hear yourself? Dude, she is the victim, and you had no right to put your hands on her. You could have killed her."

"I didn't though and had her punk ass landlord stayed out of our business, I wouldn't be in this predicament. Y'all act like people don't have disagreements."

"Disagreements?" he yells. "Andre, look at these." He slaps pictures down on the desk. "Look at them." He orders. "Is this what you call a disagreement?"

I push them away and he shakes his head.

"I admit things went too far, but I don't deserve what's happening to me. I didn't press charges on her for scratching my face."

"She was defending herself."

"Whose side are you on?" I question.

He exhales. "Dre, I think you need professional help."

I stand. "And I think the five thousand dollars you're charging should make this go away. Can't you ask for diversion or probation? I read online those are options."

"Five thousand isn't even my full rate. Nevertheless, those options aren't available when it comes to sexual assault."

"Sexual assault?" I laugh. "How can I sexually assault my girlfriend? It's called sex."

"Dude, she was unconscious when you were arrested. There's no way she could have given consent. You know this."

"Haven't you ever put your woman to sleep with some good sex?" I laugh.

"You need to take this seriously and as your attorney, I'm advising you to at least think about negotiating a plea deal. If convicted, you could face up to fifteen years on the assault and at least fifteen on the rape. Right now, they're offering three on the assault and ten on the rape to run concurrently."

"No way. I'm not taking a plea. You may as well remove that from your vocabulary. Can we go? I have stuff to do today."

"Yeah." He sighs.

Inside the courthouse, we get off the elevator and I see Ava standing near the entrance of the courtroom with another lady. I lean against the wall.

"Look at me Ava." I whisper. "Look at me."

"Andre." Langston calls out.

I tear my eyes away from her to see him waving me into the courtroom.

"All rise." The bailiff orders.

"Thank you. Please be seated." The Judge states taking her seat. "We're here today on docket number

2021BR491290, the case of Ava Gentry versus Andre Powell to extend the order of protection. Are you Ava?"

"Yes, your honor."

"And you're Andre, I presume?"

"Yes." I reply.

"Great. I'll ask for each of the attorneys to introduce yourselves, please."

"Good morning, your honor. My name is Jamia Dubose representing Ms. Gentry."

"Your honor, I'm Langston Abernathy on behalf of Mr. Powell."

"Very well. Ms. Dubose, you may call your first witness."

"Thank you. I'd like to call the petitioner, Ms. Gentry."

I watch Ava take the stand and be sworn in.

"Please state your name for the record."

"My name is Ava Gentry."

"Ms. Gentry, will you state your relationship to Mr. Powell." Her lawyer request.

"We've been in a relationship the past thirteen years."

"But you're not married?"

"No ma'am."

"Any children?"

"No."

"Can you please tell us about the events that led you to request an order of protection?"

She takes a deep breath.

"A little over two weeks ago, I came home from church to find Mr. Powell inside my house."

"Did you invite him?"

"No. We were not living together, and I did not give him a key. I believe he gained access through the back door."

"What happened then?"

"He stated he'd given me enough time to get myself together and come back to him. The conversation went on for about twenty minutes with him accusing me of cheating and saying things like I belonged to him. I'd had enough and asked him to leave. I opened the door to let him out and he," she pauses, twisting in the chair. "He um, he grabbed me by the neck lifting me from the floor. Somehow, we fell and when he released me, I tried to get my cell phone, but he grabbed me by the hair. The last thing I remember is being punched. I woke up in the hospital."

"Did you sustain any injuries?"

"Bruised ribs, a cut on my nose, two black eyes, swollen neck and broken blood vessels in my face and neck. I was also raped."

"Your honor, I'd like to enter into evidence these photos taken at the hospital the night of the incident as the petitioner's exhibit one and a copy of the doctor's report from the sexual assault exam as exhibit two."

"Any objection Mr. Abernathy?"

"No your honor."

"Why do you need this order of protection?" her attorney asks.

"To keep him away from me."

"Is this the first time he's been abusive?"

"Objection, your honor. There were no previous incidents listed on the petition and therefore should not be heard."

"I agree Ms. Dubose. Let's stick to the facts on the petition today."

"Ms. Gentry, were the police called to the scene?"

"Yes."

"Is Mr. Powell facing any charges?" she asks.

"Yes. Aggravated Domestic Assault and Rape."

"Were there any witnesses?"

"Not to the actual assault. I was told my landlord showed up afterwards."

"Are you fearful of Mr. Powell?"

"Fearful he'll try to harm me again, yes but I'm not scared of him." She looks at me.

"Your honor, no further questions."

"Mr. Abernathy, would you like to cross?" the judge asks.

He looks at me and I shake my head no.

"No your honor."

"Ms. Gentry, you may step down."

"Ms. Dubose, do you have any other witnesses?"

"Yes, your honor. We'd like to call Lt. Josiah Rainey."

I roll my eyes as the good boy cop walks into the courtroom.

"Bitch ass." I whisper and Langston kicks my foot.

He's sworn in and goes on and on like he's a knight in armor. I stare him down the entire time, not hearing anything he says.

"No further questions, your honor."

"Mr. Abernathy."

"I only have one question. Mr. Rainey, are you and Ms. Gentry involved in a romantic relationship?"

"No sir, but I don't see how that's relevant to the case at hand. Your client assaulted—

"Thank you." My attorney interrupts and he laugh. "No further questions."

"Ms. Dubose, do you have any other witnesses?"

"No, your honor."

"Very well. Mr. Abernathy, is your client going to testify?"

"No your honor. I've advised him to invoke his rights under the fifth amendment due to his pending criminal case."

"Do either of the attorneys have anything else they'd like to present?"

"No, your honor." They both respond.

"Based on the evidence presented including the testimony, I find Ms. Gentry's testimony credible, and she's met her burden of proof for me to grant her order of protection to expire twelve months from this date. Mr. Powell, this order of protection advises you to stay away from Ms. Gentry. You are to have no direct or indirect contact with her of any kind which includes in person, phone or electronically. You are not to threaten or assault her in any way. You are also hereby ordered to get rid of all firearms in your possession within 48 hours. Violating any condition of this order will have you back in jail. Do you understand?"

I stare at her.

"I'll ensure he does." Langston states.

"I'll ask that Mr. Powell exits the courtroom first to the left, Ms. Gentry to the right and I'll have a deputy bring out the signed order in a few minutes. Does either party have any questions?"

"No, your honor."

"Thank you and best of luck to both."

"This is bullsh—

"Dre, watch your mouth."

"Man, Ava know I'm not a threat to her. I made a mistake." I say loud enough for her to hear when she walks out. "You didn't have to do this."

"Andre, stop before you're violated."

I hit the wall.

"I've already lost my badge, what more does she want."

"She didn't do this to you and the quicker you realize it, the better." He says shaking his head. "Just leave the woman alone, get this criminal case resolved and move on with your life."

chapter thirty-eight
Ava

"Ava."

"Josiah. I didn't know you would be here." I give him a hug. "Thank you for not only today, but for everything."

"No problem. I'm only glad to help." He looks back at Andre. "He deserves every bit of punishment."

"I agree."

"How are you?"

"Getting better with each day. It doesn't hurt as much to breathe."

"Good."

His radio crackles before dispatch radios for him.

"Are you going to be okay getting home?" he asks.

"Yes, thank you."

"Okay. Take care and if you need anything, call."

He gives me another hug before leaving.

I turn to see Andre staring. He mouths, I'm sorry and I roll my eyes.

"Forget him." Jamia says grabbing my arm. "I have something to distract you for a moment. I received the final order from the arbitration with Ruthie and

Associates. Would you like to read it now or when we get back to the office?"

"Now, please." I hold out my hand and she gives me her phone. I scan over the document. "Nothing on the wrongful termination. Shocker." I continue reading. "Oh my God." I shriek before covering my mouth and looking at her. She smiles. "One point two million for the discrimination. Jamia." Tears rush from my eyes. "Oh my God, is this real?"

She hugs me.

"It's not as much as we asked for, but it's definitely real and they're ordered to pay all my legal fees."

"I'm happy it's finally over with. Now, let's wait and see if they actually pay."

"Oh, they will. I'm going to make sure of it."

*****

A week later, I'm in the booth of Range USA shooting the new 9MM Glock I purchased after applying for my concealed carry permit.

"Who pissed you off?" an older gentleman asks laughing when I'm pulling the paper down.

"Circumstances." I tell him.

"Well, I sho hope they get some act right cause you letting that thang rip. You in there like tah da da daaaa." He mimics my stance with sound causing me to laugh.

"I don't stand like that."

He laughs. "All I'm saying is, I don't want to be on your bad side Ms. Ma'am and whoever is, better watch out."

"I'm Ava."

"Red." He holds out his hand.

"It's nice to meet you, Red."

"The pleasure is all mine. You keep shooting like that, your circumstances won't have a choice but to change." He says walking by. "Cause won't be none left. Have a great night."

"You as well."

I pack up my things and quickly walk to my truck, getting inside making sure the doors are locked. Before I can pull off, my phone rings. I press the button to answer through the Bluetooth.

"Hello."

"Ava, please don't hang up."

"Andre, why are you calling me?"

"I'm sorry. Things got out of hand and I'm so sorry. I never meant to hurt you. Ava, you have to believe me."

"Are you crying?"

"Everything is going wrong. I lost my job, the house is a mess, my account is in the negative and I think the lights were cutoff yesterday. I don't know how to log in to pay the bills, like I have the money to pay them anyway. Ava, I messed up okay. I know I took things too far, but will you stop punishing me?"

"Oh, because I'm not around to clean your house and pay your bills, I'm punishing you? What do you call what you've done to me, huh? There's still lingering pain when I take a deep breath. When I close my eyes, I can still feel you choking me until my ears ring. I sleep with the lights on in the house because of you, yet I'm punishing you. Negro, get off my phone and don't call me again unless you want more things to go wrong."

"See, I tried to be nice and each time you take it for granted. Well, let's see who'll get the last laugh."

When he hangs up, I grab my phone to block the number. Closing my eyes, I take some deep breaths to calm myself. Preparing to drive off, the phone rings again.

Pressing the button, "Andre, I swear to God—

"Hello. Is this Ava Gentry?" the caller interrupts.

"My apologies. Who is this?"

"Hallelujah." The caller exclaims. "Ava, this is Levar Wilson from Small Sticks and I've been trying to reach you."

"Levar, hey. How are you?"

"Better now." He laughs. "I hope you don't mind, but I was able to get your contact information from a young lady who works at R&A."

"I don't, only because it sounds important. What can I do for you?"

"Would you be willing to meet me and Mike regarding a proposition we have for you? Wait, that didn't come out right. Let me start over. We'd like to offer you a job and we kind of need you to start in like three days if you're interested."

"Wow, okay." I say with some hesitancy. "What kind of job?"

"I can explain everything in person if you have some time right now."

"Um sure. Where?"

"The address is 4009 Getwell Road in Southaven, Mississippi."

I type it into the GPS. "Got it. I'm on the way."

chapter thirty-nine

Thirty minutes later, I pull up to the building, park, and Levar meets me at the door as I walk up.

"Ava, thank you for coming."

"No problem. What is this place?"

"Small Sticks." He says proudly waving his hands. "When we found out what Penelope did to you, we knew partnering with a company who shall remain nameless wasn't for us. Especially when they tried to erase everything you'd put in place. They wanted to rewrite the entire deal including removing any mention of our company's name."

"I'm not surprised they'd go back on what was agreed. I don't think they wanted to see a black company succeed which is why getting fired was a blessing in disguise."

"For both of us." He smiles.

"What do you mean?" I question.

"Them firing you showed us their true intention which led us to turning down their proposal. In doing so, God would open a door for us to receive a very large endowment from the parents of a young lady who suffers from diabetes. She saw my sister using her device at practice, one day, and the rest is history in the making."

He beams. "Due to their generosity, we were hoping, more like praying, you'd agree to becoming the head of our newly created project management department."

"Are you serious?"

"Very. Ava, based on your qualifications and the way you handled yourself while working at that nameless company, we knew you would be the best person for the position."

"I, um, I don't know what to say.

"I won't pressure you, much," he bumps my shoulder, "but allow me to show you around in the hopes of persuading you."

I laugh. "Okay."

He begins to give me a tour of the building.

"We're almost done with renovations and plan to officially open in February 2022. This area will be yours if you decide to join us. Here, you'll oversee projects within the company that you and your team will be responsible for testing and executing. Follow me.

"This is my office."

"Nice."

"Yeah, I got the opportunity to design it and I think I did pretty good." He grins. "Over here are some mockups of devices we plan to add. With your expertise and the right staff, we can keep the majority of the work inhouse.

So, Ava, do you think it's something you'd be interested in?"

"This sounds exciting, and I want to say yes, but—

"Are you concerned about the other company?"

"No. God, no. Forget them. It's just, okay." I sigh. "Being totally transparent. I recently got out of a long-term relationship and my ex is having a hard time letting go. A few weeks ago he attacked me, and we're currently involved in a criminal case which means I'll have to deal with it until it's finalized."

"Oh wow. Are you okay?"

"I'm getting there. It's just been a lot dealing with lawyers, detectives, and prosecutors all while wondering if he'll come back and praying the protection order does what it's supposed too. I'll be glad when it's over."

"I know all too well. My family and I were handed the stones of domestic violence after my sister was killed by her ex-wife last year. I can tell you, by experience, how heavy they can get. However, I'm glad you survived because many don't. Lord knows, I wish a million times over, I'd seen the signs."

He looks away.

"Many times there are no signs because the person being abused doesn't show any. I know I didn't. Although Andre had never been physically abusive, the emotional and mental was far worse. While wounds heal, words and actions stay. Yet, a person on the outside wouldn't have known."

"I'm sorry. I didn't mean to rehash all of this for you."

"Please don't apologize. It feels good to talk to someone who understands. How old was your sister?"

He picks up a picture.

"Too young to die. She'd just turned thirty and was out celebrating with some friends when the ex-wife showed up, shooting her over twenty times. When she was done, assassinating her, she stayed on the scene and waited for police. In court, she tried to claim insanity, but the jury saw through it once the evidenced proved she'd planned it. Needless to say, she was sentenced to life." He sighs rubbing the picture. "Small consolation for my sister's life, though. So, I understand if taking on a job is too much, right now. However, if you choose to come onboard, you'll become a paid employee once the paperwork is signed, officially beginning when the building opens in February. Although we'd like for you to attend a dinner meeting with us on Thursday."

"Thursday as in two days?"

"Yes. It's only a small dinner as we introduce the members of leadership."

"Can I take a day to think about it?" I ask.

"Sure thing. Here's my card. Call me either way."

"Thanks for thinking of me."

Getting to the door of his office, he turns to me. "Can I give you a hug?"

"Of course."

Before my hands go around his back, he begins to pray.

"Father, thank you for protecting Ava from the hands of the enemy. Thank you for keeping her, her mind, body, and spirit through these dark years. Father, I don't know what else you have for her, but I know she's destined to live because she's survived what should have killed her. Now God, I pray she'll have a sound mind, a renewed heart, a healed body, a steady walk, a continued perseverance to press on and strength to finish. And God, give her the courage to say yes to your will so that all the rejections she's received are eradicated from her memory. This I pray by faith, amen."

I'm sobbing into his shoulder as my arms get tighter around him. He speaks in tongue.

"God says, there will be light just as He commanded in Genesis one and fourteen. I don't know what this means to you, yet I believe God and He will perform exactly what He promised."

We stay there a few more minutes.

"I'm sorry." I tell him. "I didn't mean to cry all over you. It's just been dark for a while, and I needed that."

"There can be more if you come work with us." He winks. "I'm kidding. Seriously Ava, God hasn't forgotten you and all the tears you've shed in darkness was watering the very harvest you'll soon reap in day. Stay the course."

"I will and thank you. I'll call you." I tell him when we make it to the front door.

"Famous words when a woman didn't enjoy the first date."

I laugh.

"Drive safe Ava."

chapter forty

I stop and pick up some Beef Thai Curry from Urban Fusion. Putting my things inside the house, I open the front door to check the mailbox.

"Ava."

I jump back, raising the gun in my hand.

"Whoa. Whoa. Ava, it's Jack. I didn't mean to startle you. The door opened before I could ring the doorbell."

"I know who you are dummy. Why are you on my porch with a gift basket?"

"Can you please lower the gun?" he requests with one hand up. "Thanks. This isn't mine. It was already here."

I put the gun in the holster, snatch the basket and start to close the door.

"Wait. Will you give me the opportunity to explain?"

"Explain? Boy, if you didn't come to drop off a cashier's check then get off my property."

He holds out an envelope. I sit the basket down, take it and tear it open to see a check for the entire court ordered amount.

"I would say thank you, but it's owed. Goodbye Jack."

"I made a mistake." He blurts.

I jerk around so fast, he jumps.

"Mistake?" I laugh. "No, coward. A mistake is you coming here, again. What you did was made a choice. You chose to lie on me like I was some hoe sleeping her way to the top. You undermined everything I've worked my ass off to achieve with one lie and now you want to repent. Well trick, explain it to your priest because he probably cares about your soul, I don't. All I have for you is pity. Pity for the man you could have been had you walked your own path. Instead, you're the same cowardly lion from twenty years ago still latched to your daddy's breast. Do us both a favor. Journey down the yellow brick road to the wizard and buy your balls back."

I slam the door.

"Mane, I forgot the mail." I say when my phone rings with a Facetime call from Katrina.

"Girl, is you still in Memphis or not cause I'm trying to see." She jokes, popping her lips. "Where have you been?"

I laugh. "Baby, it's been a loooong few weeks."

"I was starting to think you'd dumped us for Anointed Temple."

"I wouldn't dare." I giggle. "I tried calling you a few times and got your voicemail. I left a message once."

"Really? I never seen any missed calls or a voicemail from you which is weird. Hmm. Anyway, is everything okay?"

"Getting there." I answer.

"You want to talk about it?"

"Give me an hour to get settled and I'll call you back."

"Of course. Talk soon." She says disconnecting.

Putting the phone on the sink, I ensure the doors are locked and the alarm armed before washing my hands and sitting down to eat. Afterwards, I shower, pour a glass of wine, get into bed and call Katrina back.

"Hey, did I catch you at a bad time?" I inquire when it connects.

"No, I was reading a book."

"What are you reading?"

"It's called Everybody Ain't Your Friend by Tanisha Stewart."

"I'll have to check her out. I used to read a lot in my free time and right now, I could use the distraction."

"Well, if you need some recommendations, let me know because there's some really good Christian Fiction authors like Khara Campbell, She Nell and D.A. Bourne on Amazon."

"Hold on." I grab my journal and pen from the nightstand and ask her to repeat the names. "Cool. Thanks."

"Now, what's been up with you. You got you a new boo or sumthin?"

I exhale looking off.

"Ava, did I say something wrong?"

"A few weeks ago, my ex broke into my home and attacked me."

She gasps.

"He left me with the prints of his fingers on my neck, bruised ribs, two black eyes and this scar across my nose." I purposely leave off the rape.

"Oh Ava. Why didn't you call me? You know I, along with the church, would have been there for you."

"I know, but truthfully I was embarrassed. Trina, this is one of the hardest things I've ever been through, and I've endured a lot. I thought I was dying, and the scariest part is knowing my death would be by the hands of someone familiar. It's like I never knew him."

"I'm so sorry you've had to endure this. Did he go to jail?"

"Yes, but he's out on bail and I have an order of protection."

"Thank God. Have you been by yourself this entire time?"

"No. I've had my best friend June and her husband along with my landlords, Josiah and Naomi. They've been a blessing for sure."

"Ava, we haven't known each other long, but I consider you a friend and if you need me, I'm here. Now, how are you and I don't want the rehearsed answer either?"

"Honestly, I'm okay, right now. Tomorrow may be totally different though."

"That's understandable because what you're going through is like grief which can sneak up on you without notice."

"Yeah, but the hardest part to overcome is the anger. One moment, I'm okay and the next, I feel like punching a hole in the wall. Sis, this man hurt me when all he had to do was walk away. It's not like he loves me. He loved what I could do for him and the first time I finally stood up for myself and told him no, he threw me out. Oh, not to mention destroying all my belongings."

"Some men are like that. They don't feel the need to get better and the whole time, you'll be getting worse because they won't treat you right, claim to not want you but refuse to let you go in order to be found my someone who does and can."

"Girl, if you didn't just preach. I mean, I begged him to let me be. It's not like either of us was happy. Then his funky face, Devin the donkey looking tail had the audacity to attack me."

She laughs. "Did you call that man Devin the donkey."

"It was better than some other things I wanted to call him." I join her laughing. "It's either laugh or let the anger from everything consume me. It seems like I can't catch a break which is causing me to second guess an amazing opportunity I received today."

chapter forty-one

"Ava, sometimes it isn't a break you need to catch because that signifies, you're waiting for luck to find you. Baby, we don't need luck, we walk by faith especially during the times darkness makes it hard to see."

"I hear you, but my flesh is having a hard time letting go. It's hard to forgive someone who intentionally hurt me, although I am trying. Every day, I'm trying." I sigh.

"It is, I can't lie. However, I've learned that trying is part of the problem." She tells me.

"Elaborate."

"Say you and I go to a restaurant because we're starving, haven't eaten all day. Looking at the menu there's something you want, but never had. The waitress comes over and gives you the option to try it. You agree and she returns with a sample, one you enjoy yet it doesn't fill you up. Why? You only tried it. Trying indicates you attempted but doing means you accomplished. Ava, truly forgiving is something you've tried but maybe never done which keeps you in this dark place shacking with fear and anger. Understand something. You have every and I mean ev-ver-ree right to be angry. You've been through more in your lifetime than one person should, but prolonged exposure to anger makes one bitter and vulnerable to the enemy."

I lean against the headboard.

"I'm sorry." She tells me.

"For what?"

"I didn't call to turn this into Bible study. I just don't want you to miss out on the next leg of your journey because of what has happened thus far. There's better for you, including a new job, happiness, wholeness and love."

"Honestly, I needed this because I've missed worship and Bible study."

"We've missed you too. Sister Edwards said she tried to call a few times without an answer."

"She may have, but with all going on, I haven't been answering a lot of unknown calls and I turned off my voicemail. Please give her my apologies."

"I will. Is it okay if I let them know you're going through something and is on the mend or would you like to keep it quiet?"

"I don't mind, but please do me one favor."

"Name it."

"Do not, in the name of all things holy, put me on the sick and prayer list." I chuckle.

"Now Ava Gentry. You know Mother Partee will have your name on that list so fast." She laughs.

"Girl, she'll have people thinking I'm in the ICU. No ma'am."

"She definitely will. And church, we need to pray for dear sister Gentry." She teases in a slow speech. "I'll make sure she doesn't."

"Please and thank you."

"Ava, in all seriousness, I'm glad you're okay. When you didn't show up to be baptized and I couldn't reach you, I knew something was wrong. If I'd known where you stayed, I would have shown up on your doorstep."

"I know and I appreciate that. Do you think Pastor Hunter will reschedule the baptism?"

"Of course. You can talk to him when you return. Oh, Sunday is women's day, and we have a dynamic speaker coming. I hope you'll be able to make it."

"I'm going to do my best. Now, speaking of better, I was offered a position with Small Sticks?"

"The one you were working with before doo-doo head lied?"

I chuckle. "Yes."

"That's awesome, isn't it?"

"It is, but I'm scared this stuff with Andre will take up too much of my time. The last thing I want is to lose another job."

"It doesn't have too. Ava, you can decide how much time you give the situation, not the other way around. Anyway, explain what's going on to your new boss. I'm sure he'll understand."

"I did and he does."

"Then what's the holdup?" she questions.

"Fear." We both say.

"Fear is a funky face liar." She speaks in tongue. "Thank you, Holy Spirit. God has given me power to adjudicate your case and I decree tonight, at 8:37 PM, your divorce from fear and flesh final. You don't need alimony, and they can keep the house because God says He'll restore everything they took. All you need is your name. Hold on." She lays the phone down.

A few minutes later she returns. "Baby, I done got happy. The name Ava Biblically means living one. The Latin form of the Hebrew Eve and just like Eve, you may have made some mistakes, yet you can still go on to change history. You may have made decisions that affected your life, in a bad way, but there's still glory available after. Shoot, God gave Eve power in spite of what she did, and that blemish didn't stop nothing. He gave her power to step on the head of the very enemy who tried her. Ava Gentry, living one, it's time you lived. Your ex may have tried, but he failed and now God is given you the power to crush his head. Maybe not physically, yet you get what I mean."

"Did you just preach on a Tuesday night?"

"Why yes, yes I did, and you can send your offering to my Cash App, dollar sign sis preaching."

I laugh. "Seriously Katrina. Thank you. God has really been showing out with the people He's surrounding me with and I'm grateful. You're also right. It's time I started living up to my name."

"Amen and hallelujah."

"Now, let me tell you about my boss and how this man prayed for me."

"Say whattttt? Spill it sis."

chapter forty-two

"So what happens now?" I ask Jamia.

"Since he waived his right to a preliminary hearing and asked for a speedy indictment, the prosecutors will now present their evidence to a grand jury who'll decide whether or not there's enough evidence to move ahead. Once an indictment is handed down, a trial date will be set unless a deal is made."

"A deal? He can actually get a deal?"

"Sure, yet it doesn't mean he'll accept." She tells me.

"What kind of deal will they offer him?"

She sighs.

"Just tell me."

"The prosecutor originally offered three on the assault and ten on the rape to run concurrently which means he'll have to serve the full thirteen. However, he turned it down. His lawyer reached out to negotiate again and the offer this time is twelve years at thirty percent and a ten thousand dollar fine if he pleads guilty. Otherwise, they'll go to trial."

"Thirty percent is what, three and a half years?"

"Unfortunately." She replies.

"Wow. How soon will we know?"

"Next week, at the latest."

"Thanks Jamia."

"No problem. I'll call with any updates."

"Wait, Jack dropped off a check the other night."

"I know. His lawyer came to see me to also drop off a check for the legal fees. Dude was mad too."

"Good. Serves them right. Can I deposit it?"

"What you said." She laughs. "And yes, you can deposit it. There is a form you'll need to sign affirming you received it, but you can stop by any time to do that. Depending on your bank, it will probably take up to ten days for it to clear though."

"No, he didn't." I blurt.

"Who is he and what did he do?" Jamia questions. "Ava, is something wrong?"

"I'm sorry to blurt that out in the middle of the conversation. There was a basket on my doorstep Tuesday night, and I sat it by the door without looking at it until now. I think it's from Andre."

"Are you sure it's from him? Is there a card?"

"Um," I search. "No, but I know it's from him. It has all my favorite snacks and a DVD of Pretty Woman."

"Send me a picture and I'll call the district attorney to see what we can do."

Some hours later, after a shower and getting dressed, I stand looking at myself in the mirror. Two years ago, I was a size twenty, sometimes twenty-two and very unhealthy. The weight was also another reason I stayed attached to Andre. Being that size, my confidence was at the lowest and I didn't think I could do any better. Truthfully, he drilled it into my head I wouldn't, and I believed it. It would take an embarrassing purchase of two plane tickets for a work trip to change things. I vowed, on those eight hours I had to think, to never be that size again. With the help of eating right and working out, I was able to lose and keep off over sixty pounds.

Lately, with all the stress and free time to work out, I've been able to lose another twenty. I rub my hand over my stomach, twisting and turning smiling at the reflection I'm falling in love with before applying lip gloss and putting my new braids into a bun.

Tonight, I'm headed to a dinner celebrating the opening of Small Sticks since I agreed to the position. Parking, I sit looking at the house, nerves taking over.

"You got this Ava." I coach myself out the truck before walking inside.

"Ma'am, may I take your jacket?" a young man asks.

"Oh." I jump. "Sure."

"There are drinks and appetizers straight ahead. Dinner will start in thirty minutes." He advises.

"Thank you."

I go over to the bar and order a glass of red wine.

"You must be Ava?" a woman says as the glass touches my lips.

"Hmm. Yes." I reply dabbing my mouth with a napkin. "Hi."

"I didn't mean to interrupt mid sip." She smiles. "Hi, my name is Larissa Stanton, Michael's wife. Levar speaks highly of you, and I wanted to welcome you to the Small Sticks family."

"Thank you. I'm excited to be a part of such an amazing company."

"Levar should be here soon. If you want, I can introduce you to everybody."

"That would be great."

"As I stated, I'm Michael's wife and the head of marketing. This is Felecia, head of Human Resources and her husband Calvin, our IT guru. This is Sonya, head of accounting and her husband Marlow. We've yet to recruit him over to our side." She pushes him.

"I'm loving the tribe of women." I smile.

"Yass girl." Felecia says giving me a fist bump.

"James Brown said it best. It's a man's world but wouldn't be nothing without a woman or a girl." Marlow sings.

"Say that bae." Sonya snaps says causing everybody to laugh.

"Yeah, the men are definitely outnumbered." Michael states walking in.

"You wouldn't have it any other way." Larissa smiles when he comes over putting his arm around her.

"Ava, we're honored to have you onboard. Thank you for saying yes and coming tonight." Michael tells me.

"It's good to see you again and I appreciate you all giving me a chance."

Another couple comes in and she introduces me to Mr. and Mrs. Abraham and Tiffany Young, those who donated the money. I gush over the fact they're black, educated, and prosperous.

"It's very nice to meet you, Ava." Tiffany says.

"You as well. You both have a beautiful home."

"This is all Abraham's doing. I'd be content with a three bedroom, two bath on a whole lot of land."

"Says the woman who has every room occupied. Ava don't listen to her. She'd be lost without all the space." Abraham jokes.

"He's right, but I'll never admit it." She whispers.

"Dinner is ready." Someone announces.

chapter forty-three

We take our seats at the table as Levar rushes in.

"While you're up, say a few words and bless the food." Michael tells him.

"Really dude." He rolls his eyes. "Good evening, everybody. Please forgive my tardiness. First, I must begin by thanking God. It's because of Him, Michael and I were able to write and continually execute the vision of Small Sticks. We had hopes of one day becoming a household name and now with the generosity of Abraham and Tiffany Young, along with a dynamic team we have that opportunity. Small Sticks started off as the dream of two college roommates who were tired of seeing their loved ones struggling to do the very thing needed to help them live. Although it has taken a long three years, this is only the beginning. I don't know what all God has planned for us, but I pray it only gets better for each of us in the room. Abraham and Tiffany, I pray your cups are never empty and God repays your generosity and faith in us."

Michael stands. "I ditto everything Levar has said. This was all a dream." He sings. "That was my channeling Tupac Shakur." He laughs. "In all seriousness, it has taken and will take a lot of work, yet I believe in what we've created. All we need now, is the help of each of you in this room. To my wife Larissa who has stood by my side believing and speaking life into this dream even when it didn't look like things would work out. Baby, I love you and I promise, I'm going to take you on that vacation you've been dreaming of soon. To each of you who make up Small Sticks, Abraham, and Tiffany, thank you for taking the chance with us. It may start off turbulent and take some long days and nights, but it'll all be worth it. All we ask is for your trust, dedication, work and prayers."

He nods at Levar.

"Shall we pray. God, thank you again for your grace and mercy. God, as we prepare to dine, bless the food as we eat and bless the family in the seat. Bless the hands of the cooks and the Youngs for the table, may you continually shine your light to let us know you're able. Bless the fellowship among friends and may the love and relationships never end. Amen."

"Amen."

"Boy, we didn't know you were a poet too." Marlow jokes and he throws a roll at him.

We spend the next two hours eating and talking before moving to their outside patio for cocktails and cigars.

The song *Running out of Lies* by *Johnnie Taylor* plays and Abraham begins to sing and dance with Tiffany.

"You can rest assured my woman's no fool. She can tell I been loving you. Stealing your love is getting harder and harder, the excuses I been giving just won't hold water."

"What do you know about Johnny?" Levar asks when he sees me singing.

"I grew up listening to my granddaddy playing these kinds of songs." I laugh. "Those were the good days."

"So, are you telling me you know about the blues?"

"Of course. Tyrone Davis, Denise Lasalle and Bobby Womack are a few of my favorites."

"Grown folk music." We both say together.

"They don't make music like this anymore. What about you? Who are some of your favorites?" I ask.

"I'm more of a Luther Vandross, Teddy Pendergrass, and O'Jays type of guy."

"Okay. I'm with it, but only if it's big Luther."

"Ah, I feel you. Let me see what I can come up with." He goes over to the entertainment center.

A minute later, *Never Too Much* by *Luther Vandross* plays. He comes back holding out his hand.

"Can I have this dance?"

"You can."

Some hours later, Levar walks me out.

"I don't know the last time I've had this much fun. Thank you."

"No thanks needed. Ava, we're happy to have you as part of our family. Thank you for saying yes. By the way, you look absolutely beautiful tonight."

"Thank you. You're not bad yourself."

"Drive safe." He starts to walk off then stops. "Will it be too uncomfortable to ask for a text when you make it home?"

"Not at all."

He smiles, closing my door. I watch him walk back to the sidewalk. He turns and waves.

Getting home, I lock up the house and set the alarm. In my bedroom, I text Levar. Seconds later he responds.

Levar Wilson: Dang girl, either you stay close, or you have a heavy foot.

Me: All you need to know is, I made it safe sir. 😌 😂

Levar Wilson: Okay Dalesha Earnhardt.

Me: Dalesha, really? 😑

Levar Wilson: Welp if the pedal fits 🚲 . Thank you for letting me know you made it.

Me: LOL. I'll let you have that one. Have you made it home?

Levar Wilson: Yes, a few minutes ago.

Me: Good. Thanks again for tonight and taking a chance on me.

Levar Wilson: You didn't need a chance Ava, only a change. Everything you need is already inside of you.

Me: 💜 Goodnight

Levar Wilson: Say your prayers and sleep tight.

Laying the phone down, I smile. "Lord, if only I'd met him fourteen years ago."

chapter forty-four

"You are my strength. Strength like no other. Strength like no other, reaches to me. In the fullness of your grace. In the power of your name. You lift me up. You lift me up." The choir sings before the leader goes into Nobody like you Lord. People in the congregation cry out.

"Anybody need God this morning like never before? Anybody ever found themselves in a place where nobody could help or console you but God? Anybody in the house?" she asks.

I lift my hands.

"Somebody tell God this morning, fill me up til I overflow."

"God, fill me up til I overflow." I repeat.

"Maybe it's just me who needs God's power to fall on me like rain. Maybe it's just me who've found myself on the receiving end of pain more times than I can keep count of. Maybe it's just me who've been hurt and let down by folk you thought you could trust. Oh, but one thing I know for sure there's nobody like my God. Oh!" She cries out. "Nobody like you God."

"There's nobody like God." The morning speaker says once at the podium. "A God who wakes us up even when we don't thank Him for laying us down. A God who will protect us from danger we didn't even realize we were in. Anybody willing to tell God thank you? Thank you, God for keeping me when I was a raggedy mess, unworthy of your forgiveness, too blinded by sin to see you and too distracted by flesh to hear you. Thank you, God. Whew. Okay, I'm going to leave that alone. Oh, but when I think of the goodness of Jesus and all He's done for me, my soul and mouth cry out hallelujah. Okay. Okay. Take your seats."

She waits until it settles.

"Please go with me to a familiar passage of scripture, Hebrews chapter twelve, verses one and two. I'm reading from the New American Standard Bible. Bible says, *"Therefore, since we also have such a great cloud of witnesses surrounding us, let's rid ourselves of every obstacle and sin which so easily entangles us, and let's run with endurance the race that is set before us, looking only at Jesus, the originator and perfector of the faith, who for the joy set before Him endured the cross, despising the shame, and has sat down at the right hand of the throne of God."* For those looking for a subject, it's called, I changed my mind."

She pauses.

"We're living in times when chaos and confusion, evilness, suicides, murders, abuse, etc. is on the rise which says to me, it's not the time for us to be quiet. Every morning we should get up thankful for making it. I know somebody is inwardly thinking, what's there to be thankful for when you have more bills than money, sickness, loneliness, grief, and low self-esteem. Pastor lady, why should I be excited about seeing this day when it's just as hard as yesterday? Well, I'll tell you. It's because you have witnesses who can testify, it won't always be like this.

See, I was excited about the themed scripture in Hebrews twelve for women's day because God would use me to speak hope to my sisters. Sisters who are often overlooked but overworked. Underpaid, but over needed. The sisters who are tired of having to control our feelings or we're deemed emotional. Those of us who are sick of having to prove who we are because Negros are threatened by our gifts. We're criticized differently when we have a baby out of wedlock, deemed angry when what we are is tired.

Tired of being called bitter when what we are is unhealed from burdens people don't think we carry. Tired of having to fight, day in and day out, to prove our worth to folk who couldn't afford us no way. Tired of having to validate our skills and anointing. Tired of keeping quiet because you don't know how to accept or handle us. Tired of hushing and simply handling. Far too long, as women, we've forfeited stuff because we were distracted by fear, self-doubt, self-sabotage, unworthiness, lies, mistakes, the past, regret, and etc.

Well, no more. Today we're letting hell, abusers, the enemy, his imps, the workers of darkness, those who doubted us, those who left us, those who lied on us, those who took advantage of us, those who said we wouldn't be nothing, those who always got something negative to say, those who thought; yeah, we came to let them know we're changing our mind.

See, a lot of us have been distracted by stuff and people who's playing with our emotions, smothering our sound, victimizing our voice, causing us to challenge our calling and question who we are. When we do this, we'll find ourselves opposing God's promise for our life. God, why did you make me like this? God, are you sure I'm the right woman for the assignment? God, why this or that? And all the time we're spending questioning, we're being distracted from the very thing God has called us to do.

Well, we're changing our mind. Yeah, we're going to do like the author of Hebrews twelve since we're surrounded by such a huge crowd of witnesses to the life of faith, we're going to strip off every weight that slows us down, especially the sin that so easily trips us. Instead, we're going to run with endurance the race God has set before us like it's already won. We're going to lay aside every weight we've become comfortable in and the sin we keep creating entanglements with, in order to run the race God has set before us.

Somebody, in this house, needs to declare I'm going to remove every weight that's been causing me to stagger and slow down, because I've got a race to run. I'm going to get rid of every weight that's been causing me to wobble and delay, because I've got a race to run. I'm taking off every weight. Worry, Excuse, Iniquity, Guilt, Hindrance and Transgression that's been causing me to forfeit my race because if I never run, how will I know I can win.

You don't have to trust me because I've got some witnesses who've run before me, and their story gives me hope to keep running even when I find it hard to breathe from tiredness and it seems like it's in vain. Come here Rachel, a woman who couldn't do the very thing she'd watched sisters and concubines do, bare children. Yet Bible shares in *Genesis 30:22, "Then God remembered Rachel's plight and answered her prayers by enabling her to have children."* She's a witness to how prayer works.

Come here Hannah. Womb shut, spent days and nights being bullied by Peninnah, crying out to God and He was silent, accused of being drunk by the Bishop, yet she pressed. And when God remembered her, Bible shares in *1 Samuel 1:20, "and in due time she gave birth to a son."* She is a witness of God's promise. Come here woman disabled for eighteen years. Jesus saw her in the synagogue, called her over and set her free. Bible shares in *Luke 13:13, "Then He placed His hands on her, and immediately she straightened up and began to glorify God."* She's a witness to God's power as Jehovah Rapha, The Lord our Healer.

Samaritan woman at the well who'd been let down and passed over by men. Probably laughed at and shunned by women, yet she sat down and had a conversation with Jesus. It didn't matter about her past, it was her present state Jesus concerned Himself with. Because He did, she came to the well shamed, but left shouting, *"Come, see a man who told me everything I ever did. Could this be the Christ?"* She's a witness to God's love. This is why, I'm laying aside every weight and I'm going to now run with endurance the race God has set before me. Well, how do you do that Pastor? By keeping my eyes on Jesus."

chapter forty-five

After the benediction, I look around for Katrina and see her up front. I go up, touching her arm. She turns around, squealing then hugging me.

"I'm so happy to see you." She tells me.

"Ava, Katrina told us you'd been ill." Lady April Hunter says after giving me a hug. "How are you?"

"Much better, thank you and I apologize for not contacting the church."

"No apology needed. We're happy you're okay and when you're ready to reschedule your baptism, please let me know." Pastor Hunter adds shaking my hand.

"Pastor, with everything that has happened, sooner the better works for me." I chuckle.

"Then next Sunday it is. Take care and if there's anything you need from us, don't hesitate to call."

"Yes sir."

"Ava, this is Pastor Tanya Little." Katrina introduces.

"Pastor Little, your message this morning was right on time. Thank you." I tell her.

"To God be the glory." She steps closer. "Ava, sometimes the road ahead looks dark, unleveled, fill with twists and turns, hills and more road than you think you have strength to run; yet if you trust in the ability God created within you, you'll find your second wind. Keep running Ava."

"I will."

"Where are you headed, want to get some lunch?" I ask Katrina.

"Ugh, I have an open house this afternoon. You want to come with me?"

"Nah, I'll pick up some takeout and head home. You be careful and call me when you're done." I tell her.

Getting home, I walk into the kitchen and abruptly stop. My heart begins to race. The last Sunday I attended church was the same day Andre attacked me. Suddenly, the alarm begins to blare. Dropping the bag and my purse, I rush over to the keypad, punching in the code as tears spill from my eyes. Sliding down onto the floor, the nightmare of that day flashes through my mind. My breathing quickens and I grab at my chest willing myself to calm down.

Scrambling to find my phone, I unlock it, frantically opening the phone app. With my vision blurry and chest tight, I touch the screen. The volume is loud so when the call connects, I can hear.

"Ava, hey."

"I. CAN'T. BREATHE." I get out.

"Where are you?"

"Home."

"Okay, close your eyes and listen to my voice. Will you do that for me?"

"Yes."

"Good. Now, breathe for me Ava. Inhale then exhale. Good. You're okay. You're safe. You're in your home. Your home. This is your home, Ava. Breathe. Inhale then exhale."

After a few deep breaths, I open my eyes.

"Ava?"

I pick up the phone, realizing I called Levar.

"Ava, are you there?"

"Oh God, I'm sorry." I tell him through tears. "I didn't realize I'd called you."

"You don't have to apologize. Are you okay?"

"No." I admit exhaling.

"Would you like to talk about it?"

"The day I was attacked, I'd come in from church to find my ex inside my home and today was the first time going back to church since it happened. Coming home, brought back all those memories and they hit me like a ton of bricks. Man, I thought I was getting over this."

I press my head against the wall.

"Getting over what you've experienced is the hardest part and although we can wish for a timeframe of when those memories won't hurt as much, nobody can tell you that. Instead, you have to keep inhaling and exhaling until you're able to breathe without pain."

"Thank you."

"No thanks needed. Is there anything I can do?"

"You've already done it by answering the phone."

"I'll answer each time, day or night."

"Thank you, Levar."

"You're welcome. Have a great night, Ava."

"You too."

Pressing the end button, I lay the phone on the floor.

"I sought the Lord, and He answered me and delivered me from all my fears." I state. "Fear shall not be my portion." I sit there a few minutes longer before getting up, deciding I will not be afraid in my own home.

The following Monday, I stop by the bank and deposit the check before going by Jamia's office.

"Hey." She motions for me to come in. "Give me a second to get the paper. How are you?"

"I'm okay. How are you?"

"Girl, I'm far better than blessed. Oh, I heard from the District Attorney's office. One, without solid proof of

Andre sending the basket, they couldn't revoke his bond. Two, he declined the deal."

"Figured as much. What happens next?"

"Since he was indicted by the grand jury, he had to turn himself in and post bond again. At this point, the prosecutor will set a date for trial. Although I really thought he'd take the deal seeing he could potentially get twenty years if convicted."

"You don't know Andre." I tell her. "He thinks he's going to beat this."

"We'll the evidence says otherwise. Anyway, Davis at the prosecutor's office will keep me updated because you'll need to meet with them while they prepare. Once I hear anything, I'll let you know. Here's the paper." She places it in front of me. "This says you've received the settlement check and will not be going after Ruthie and Associates for further damages. It also includes a clause stating this settlement is closed and confidential and if you share it with anyone, outside of those involved, they have the right to sue."

"Child." I roll my eyes taking the pen, signing, and dating the document. "Good riddance."

"Do you have any plans for the money?" she inquires.

"Yeah, I'm going to tithe, build a house, take a vacation, invest and enjoy the rest."

"Sounds like a great plan to me."

"Jamia, thank you for everything."

"No problem. You know I got you. Take care Ava and I'll be in touch."

chapter forty-six

Friday evening, I'm in the office with Levar, Michael, and Larissa as we work on the marketing plan for the upcoming release of Small Sticks' signature USB, they've named Buddi with an I.

"Why Buddi?" I question.

"Michaiah." Michael and Larissa say at the same time.

"Michaiah is our seven-year-old." Michael continues. "She was four when she was diagnosed with diabetes. She hated getting her finger stuck and having to sit still while we worked to get enough blood on the testing strip then into the cartridge. It was too much. One night, Levar and I, were brainstorming ideas when I accidently broke a USB inside the port on my laptop. Crazy, but looking at it, we started sketching out an idea for a compact testing device. After all the work and paperwork, we created our first mockup. She called it Buddi, and it stuck."

"So, I was thinking about that." Larissa says. "Buddy is defined as a close friend, right. Why not market it as Buddy & I which equals Buddi? We can create different carrying cases like the ones we see for Air Pods thus giving each person their own little "buddi,"" she puts in air quotes.

"I like that." Levar adds. "And it won't be geared only towards children, but adults as well."

"Right."

"Ava, can you work with Danny in engineering to sketch out some ideas for the cases and maybe get a few mockups created?"

"Of course." I open my email and send him a message.

"Great work. Let's call it a night."

"Ava, we're headed to Lottie's for some karaoke and grown folk juice, if you'd like to join us." Larissa offers.

"Sure."

An hour later we walk into Lottie's. The hostess leads us to a booth close to the stage. When I see Chuck and Marcia standing near the bar, I excuse myself and go over to them. Coming back to the table, I order a strawberry lemonade vodka and an order of wings.

"Okay, who's going to be the first to do karaoke?" Larissa looks at me.

"Oh no. I'm going to need some of that grown folk juice before I commit to that." I laugh.

"I'm going to hold you to it."

We make small talk until the server comes over with our appetizers followed by Chuck.

"I hope you all are enjoying Lottie's." He states. "Ava, are you going to grace the stage tonight?"

"Aw naw." Larissa jokes. "Don't tell us you're a regular karaoker."

"Karaoker?" I laugh. "Did you just make that up?"

"I did, but don't change the subject."

"No. I've only done it once." I swat at Chuck. "You didn't have to tell my business."

"My bad. She's really good." He adds rushing away.

I turn to all of them looking at me.

"It was one time and let's just say, I don't remember much about it. However, I may do one song tonight. Just one though."

Coming out of the bathroom, I run into Dr. Greene who's getting alcohol from the storage closet.

"Hey, you need some help?" I question.

"Hey Ava, sure." She hands me a few bottles. "How are you?"

"I'm good and you?"

"Great. It's good to see you smiling."

"Thank you. I'm finding my way to happiness, even if the journey to get there is bumpy."

"It's not always about the journey, but the destination."

"Amen to that." I hand her the bottles once we're at the bar.

"Thank you for the help."

"You're welcome and I'll see you next week."

I laugh walking back to the table at Larissa who's on stage singing her heart out to Cyndi Lauper's, Girls Just Want to Have Fun.

"Are you okay?" Levar leans over and asks.

"Yeah. I was talking to Marcia. She and her husband Chuck are the owners of Lottie's and she's also my therapist."

"A licensed therapist or bartender-therapist?" He smiles bumping my shoulder.

"Both, I guess you could say however I'm seeing the licensed version."

"Cool."

We turn our attention to Larissa, clapping and cheering when the song is over.

"That was fun." She squeals sliding into the booth. "Ava, you've got to do it."

"I might." I reply as the hostess calls Levar up.

"Oh, I've got to see and hear this."

The music starts and my eyes widen at his voice as he sings Take You Out by Luther Vandross.

"She caught me by surprise, I must say 'cause I never have seen such a pretty face. With such a warm and beautiful smile, it wasn't hard for me to notice her style. I was fascinated, surely. She took my heart and held it for me. I wouldn't let her get away not until she heard me say. Excuse me miss, but what's your name? Where are you from and can I come and possibly, can I take you out tonight? To a movie, to the park, I'll have you home before it's dark so let me know, can I take you out tonight?"

Larissa clears her throat looking at me. "Um, could he be asking you out via song ma'am?"

All I do is smile while my stomach has butterflies, and my heart races.

When the song is over, he returns to the table.

"Really dude?"

"What? I know it wasn't big Luther, but it's a good song." He laughs.

"Seriously, you can sing." I tell him. "That was great."

"Thank you. Ava, I—"

"Next up, Ava." The hostess says and I look at Larissa who has a big smile on her face.

"You said one song."

I slowly slide out of the booth and over to the computer. Finding the song, I press play and go up to the microphone.

Exhaling, I let the intro to *Deborah Cox's Nobody's Supposed to Be Here* play before beginning to sing.

"I've spent all my life on a search to find, the love who'll stay for eternity. The heaven sent to fulfill my needs but when I turned around again love has knocked me down. My heart got broken. Oh, it hurt so bad. I'm sad to say love wins again. So I place my heart under lock and key to take some time and take care of me, but I turn around and you're standing here."

Once the song is over, I stop by the bar for a bottle of water before sliding back into my seat.

"Oh no ma'am." Larissa states. "You ain't gone just slide yo tail into this booth like you didn't kill that song."

I sip the water.

"I'm shook." She laughs. "You and Levar, just know we're definitely doing this again."

"For now, we have to go and relieve the babysitter, or my wife would be back on that stage." Michael says grabbing her purse.

I look at my watch and see it's after ten.

"Y'all can go ahead, I'll walk Ava out." Levar tells them.

"Cool. See y'all Monday."

"My apologies if I overstepped." He tells me.

"No, it's okay. I'm ready when you are." Grabbing my things, I wave goodbye to Chuck and Marcia. Stopping at the driver's side door, I turn to him. "I had a great time and I need to thank you for the other day. I hope it didn't make things weird between us."

"It didn't for me, what about you?"

"Well, I was a little embarrassed to be crying and hyperventilating to my boss."

"Can't we also be friends?" he inquires.

I pause.

"I understand if it's too soon."

"No, it's not." I correct. "I'd like that."

"Then you have nothing to be embarrassed about."

I press to unlock the door and he opens it.

"Drive safe and let me know you made it home."

"Were you asking me out?" I blurt.

"Was it that obvious?" he laughs.

"Yeah, it was, but the answer is no."

His mouth forms an o.

"Levar, I like you and I don't want to risk cutting you with the parts of me still broken or us getting involved because we share a common trauma. Not saying what you had planned was anything more than a simple date, yet I need to find Ava and I don't know how long this reconstruction process is going to take. Nevertheless, it would be selfish of me to ask you to wait."

"I understand and honestly, I'm happy you said no."

"Why?" I question confused.

"Because I don't want to be the one who derails you from all God is going to do for you. However, when the dust settles and the reconstruction is over, I'm coming for you."

He walks over and kisses me on the cheek.

I stare at him.

"I said what I said. Now, get in the truck woman and text me when you make it home."

chapter forty-seven

Sunday morning, I'm preparing to leave the house when I get a text from an unsaved number.

(901) 626-9999: Congratulations on finally getting baptized. Hopefully the water doesn't start boiling when you step in.

I shake my head, blocking the number and deleting the text. "Get under my feet Satan."

An hour later, I'm standing in the waiting area outside of the baptism pool. I close my eyes to pray.

"Lord, I've spent too many years without you and today I begin again with you. Please forgive me for the unbelief, tardiness, doubt, and my inability to see you beyond my flesh. God, you have my permission to have your way, allowing the Holy Spirit to inhabit every area within me. I am yours and I believe, help my unbelief. In Jesus' name, amen."

"Amen."

I turn to see Katrina, eyes full of tears. She rushes over to give me a hug. "I'm so proud of you."

"Thank you."

One of the deacons begins to read First Peter, chapter three starting at verse eight and I walk to the door. Another deacon reaches out his hand to help me inside.

"...baptism now saves you—not the removal of dirt from the flesh, but an appeal to God for a good conscience—through the resurrection of Jesus Christ, who is at the right hand of God, having gone into heaven, after angels and authorities and powers had been subjected to Him." He recites.

Pastor Hunter places his hand around my back. "God, in His infinite wisdom has allowed us to join together to witness the baptism of you, Ms. Ava Gentry. Lord, we know without you this water holds no power, yet we rejoice today knowing you stirred it the moment Ava's foot touched it. So, now God we declare like Acts twenty-two and sixteen that Ava shall rise, baptized and her sins washed away because she called on your name. Therefore, I baptize you my sister, in the name of the Father, Son and Holy Spirit."

Coming up, I lift my hands into the air crying out. "Hallelujah. God, thank you for waiting on me."

Pastor Hunter hugs me before I'm helped out. Walking into the room, I gasp, ugly crying at the sight of Katrina, June, Grant, Josiah, Naomi, Levar, Larissa, and Michael.

"Y'all." Is the only word I can form properly.

June wraps a towel around me as they form a circle.

"God, we thank you. We thank you Father for your grace and mercy. We thank you for the chance to begin again and the love you give in abundance. Today, God, we pray for this new beginning of Ava's life. We pray the spirit will fall upon her like it did Jesus. We pray you'll continue to protect, provide, and keep her even more now." June gets emotional.

Josiah continues. "Thank you, Father for allowing her to get here. We may not know all she's had to overcome, yet we won't harp over what has been. Instead God, we'll look ahead to what will be. Love, prosperity, peace, joy, hope, strength, and your promise. Father, deal with her enemies, reposition the hedge of protection around her, and let her always see the friends, new and old, you have placed in her life. We love you God and believe you'll do what you promised. In Jesus name, amen."

"I don't know what to say. I've never had this," I motion to the circle, "and to know each of you would be here for me means more than words. Thank y'all."

"We wouldn't miss being here for you." Levar touches my chin and smiles.

"He's right." Grant adds. "We're family."

"We'll let you get dressed and will see you after service." Larissa says.

Once service is over, I meet everyone in the vestibule where I give each of them a hug. June made reservations for brunch at a restaurant called Biscuits & Jam.

"I'm going by the bathroom then I'll meet you at the car." I tell them headed to the bathroom with Katrina behind me.

"I hope the food is good. I'm starving." I remark as we each go into the stall.

"Me too." A few seconds later, I hear her talking. "Yes. Hey. No, we're headed to brunch but let me call you right back. Yeah, I answered through my Air Pod. Okay. Bye silly."

"Bye silly." I joke.

"Oh hush." She laughs. "I'll wait for you outside." She washes her hands and goes out.

Coming out of the stall, I wash my hands. Opening the door, I walk up and see her on Facetime. I move to pass her then freeze when I hear the voice.

"Why are you talking to my ex?" I angrily ask trying to snatch the phone.

She moves. "Your ex? What are you talking about?" she looks at the phone then back to me as June comes over.

"That's Andre."

"Wait, what's going on?" June inquires.

"She's on the phone with Andre."

"Andre? No, you're mistaken. His name is Donte. Babe, tell her."

He smirks then hangs up.

"Call him back."

She does, twice and he ignores the calls.

"Do you have any pictures?"

"Yeah." She fumbles with the phone. "See."

"Boo, his name is Andre Donte Powell, a Sagittarius, date of birth is December 12, 1977, shoe size is a thirteen but don't believe the hype, he used to be a police officer with no ambition and whatever he's sold you is a lie, a bold face lie. How did you meet him?"

"No. No." She repeats. "He must look like him or something because he told me his name was Donte who I met a few months ago at a Labor Day event—

"For the police department." I finish the sentence. "That's because his name is Andre and he's a liar."

"Oh my God, I feel sick. He's been lying to me this entire time."

"Katrina, please be honest. Did you know who he was?"

"No, I swear. Why don't you believe me?" she yells causing the few people left to turn around.

"What's going on?" the rest of the group rushes over.

"Katrina is dating Andre." June tells them. "Yet, I find it funny you didn't know who he was."

"I didn't." She asserts. "I've never met him nor seen a picture and he told me his name was Donte. I don't have a reason to lie."

"Ok, calm down and lower your tone. This is still a church." Larissa states.

"I can't believe this. Do you talk about me around him?" I ask.

"Yes. You're my friend and he's my boyfriend, I didn't see anything wrong with that."

"This isn't your fault." I assure her. "I'm willing to bet he knew who you were beforehand, and all of this is a way to get back at me. It's also how he knew so much about me. Katrina, I can't tell you what to do with your life, but Andre isn't it."

"She's being too nice." June cuts in. "Andre isn't worth the dog poop on the bottom of your shoe. You can do better. However, it's your life but you got to pick sis. It's either him or Ava."

"I can't." She says through tears. "Please don't make me choose."

When I see her grip her stomach, an angry chuckle escapes my lips. "Oh my God. You're pregnant."

The end ... for now!

Thank you for reading part one of Almost Destroyed. Yes, I know ... I left you with a cliff hanger. However, I hope you've enjoyed Ava's story thus far. Although we all know this is a fictional story, I pray some parts of it has helped you in some way.

Just like Ava, you may have gone through a lot in life, unsure of your next move or the right direction. Maybe you too have dealt with the effects of Complex PTSD. Maybe you don't even realize it.

Yet, here's my prayer for you ...

Father, help the sister and/or brother who's found themselves in darkness. God, help the parts of them that have yet to heal. Help the parts of them which have been almost destroyed by abuse, self-doubt, sabotage, lies, hurt, pain and etc. God, deliver them and give them the hope to start over. And God, if they have you on hold, please don't hang up because they need you. Amen.

As always with every book, I wouldn't be Lakisha if I didn't leave you with this. If you need help, get it. Seek a licensed therapist because therapy isn't a bad thing. You deserve to be healed, happy and whole. You deserve to be free. You deserve to find you.

P.S. The sermon mentioned by Dr. Kia Moore of The Church at the Well in Memphis, TN is real, and it blessed me. I did ask her permission to include the snippet within the book, but if you want to check out the entire sermon, here - https://fb.watch/cDcHTXo_6Y/

Again, thank you for taking the time to read and support Almost Destroyed. I pray you enjoyed it. If you did, please leave a review, post it on social media (tag me) and share it with friends and family. If you're a member of a book club and would like to feature this book, email me at authorlakisha@gmail.com as I'd love to be a part of the discussion.

Again, and as always, I'm grateful each time you support me. If this is your first or twentieth time reading a book by me, THANK YOU! If we haven't connected on social media, what are you waiting for.

Twitter: _kishajohnson

Instagram: kishajohnson and DearSisVlog

Tik Tok: AuthorLakisha and _DearSis

Email: authorlakisha@gmail.com

Please check out the many other books available by visiting my Amazon Page. For upcoming contests and give-a-ways, I invite you to like my Facebook page, AuthorLakisha, join my reading group Twins Write 2 or follow https://authorlakishajohnson.com/. You can also join my newsletter by clicking visiting https://mailchi.mp/f94b5be20605/lakisha-johnson.

I promise not to bombard you.

About the Author

Lakisha has been writing since 2012 and has penned thirty novels, devotionals, and journals. You can find topics of faith, abuse, marriage, love, loss, grief, losing hope etc. on the pages of her many books.

In addition to being a self-published author, she's also a wife of 23 years, mother of 2, Grammy to one, Co-Pastor of Macedonia MB Church in Hollywood, MS; Sr. Business Analyst with FedEx, Devotional Blogger, and the product of a large family. She's a college graduate with 2 Associate Degrees in IT and a Bachelor of Science in Bible.

Lakisha writes from her heart and doesn't take the credit for what God does because if you were to strip away everything; you'd see Lakisha is simply a woman who boldly, unapologetically, and gladly loves and works for God.

Ask her and she'll tell you, "It's not just writing, its ministry."

Also available

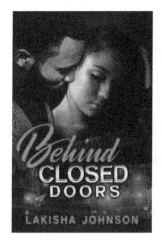

Pastor Layton and Lady Natasha Briggs were destined to marry. Well, according to their parents who arranged things before they were old enough to walk.

Now, thirteen years later, Layton and Tasha find themselves at odds. Love, honor and cherish have all been replaced with arguing, accusations, and domestic violence. A toxic environment that is tainting the heart and mind of their six-year-old daughter Lael.

Early one Sunday morning, things take a more violent turn, leaving Lael to make a 911 call that will chill the darkest of souls. Proverbs 18:22 says, "He who finds a wife finds a good thing and obtains favor from the Lord." But what happens when the love is lost and there are secrets behind closed doors?

Chance McGhee is a few months shy of her 40th birthday and marrying the man she's spent the last three years with until he dumps her two months before the wedding. Left devastated and angry, she prays telling God she'll remove her hand and wait for Him to give her another chance at love, or she's done for good.

Lauren Daniels had everything planned. She'd go to college, get the degree, settle down, get married, build her career as a sought-after architect, and have a family. For the most part, things worked accordingly. Until she decides to change the plans to get what she wants.

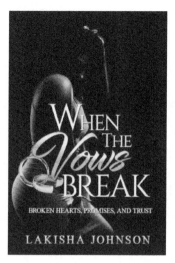

Dearly beloved, that's how it begins, what God has joined together, let no man put asunder; that's how it ends. Happily married, wedded bliss and with these rings, we do take; but what happens to happily ever after when the vows break?

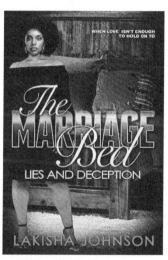

Lynn thinks their marriage bed is suffering. Jerome, on the other hand, thinks Lynn is overreacting. His thoughts, if it ain't broke, don't break it trying to fix it. Then something happens that shakes up the Watson household and secrets are revealed but the biggest secret, Jerome has, and his lips are sealed.

They say first comes love then comes ... a kidnapping, attacks, lies and affairs. Someone is out for blood but who, what, when and why? Secrets are revealed and Rylee fears for her life when all she ever wanted was not to be The Forgotten Wife.

What would you do if you woke up one morning with pain doctors couldn't diagnose, medicine couldn't minimize, sleep couldn't stop and kept getting worse?

Still Fighting is an inside look into my sister's continued fight with Trigeminal Neuralgia, a condition known as the Suicide Disease because of the lives it has taken.

Other Available Titles

A Compilation of Christian Stories: Box Set

Shattered Vows Box Set

Dear God: Hear My Prayer

2:32 AM: Losing My Faith in God

When the Vows Break 2

When the Vows Break 3

Shattered

Shattered 2

Tense

Broken

The Pastor's Admin

The Family that Lies

The Family that Lies: Merci Restored

Last Call

Covet

Chased

I'm Not Crazy

While I Slept

Wondah

Bible Chicks: Book 2

Devotionals:

Doses of Devotion

You Only Live Once: Youth Devotional

Journals:

HERoine Addict

Be A Fighter

Surviving Me

Kindle Vella:

First Lady

Made in the USA
Middletown, DE
28 March 2025

73381758R00177